I0590867

LUIS DE MIRANDA

PARIDAIZA

TRANSLATED BY TINA KOVER

THIS IS A SNUGGLY BOOK

ISBN: 978-1-64525-046-3

PARIDAIZA

LUIS DE MIRANDA, a novelist and philosopher, was born in 1971, in Portugal, and was raised and has spent most of his life in Paris. He is the author of numerous books, both fiction and non-fiction, which have won him critical praise in France. Snuggly Books published his novella *Who Killed the Poet?* in 2017. He now lives in Sweden.

TINA KOVER is the translator of more than twenty works of fiction and nonfiction. She won the 2019 Albertine Prize and the Lambda Literary Award for her translation of Négar Djavadi's Disoriental and a 2020 French Voices Award for her translation of Hervé Le Corre's In the Shadow of the Fire, and has been a finalist for the National Book Award, the PEN Translation Award, and the Warwick Prize for Women in Translation. Her translations for Snuggly Books include Luis de Miranda's *Who Killed the Poet?* and Catherine Dousteyssier-Khoze's *The Beauty of the Death Cap*.

PARIDAIZA

"Restore to them what they have lost,
They will see the harvested grain
Enclosed once again within the ear,
swaying above the grass.
Teach them, from rise to fall,
The yearly span of their faces,
They will embrace the emptiness of their hearts
until the next wanting;
For nothing sinks, or delights in ashes;
And he who knows to expect the earth's abundance
Cares nothing for failure, even when all is lost."

—René Char

Introit

"But what if the soul were just the shadow of desire?" he murmurs, pulling off his shirt.

"Then it would be noon and there would be no shadows," she retorts, defiantly, and then kisses him to make him stop talking.

"I'm the animal of desire!"

She presses a fingertip to his lips. A sort of whirlwind passes through the pitch-dark room. Has time begun to loop back on itself? The sofa-bed's springs groan as they fall onto it.

Clara's long legs, like a cosmonaut's suit-straps, beckon Nuno to hurl himself trustingly into the void. Enveloped in a halo, they hover, sighing, on the brink of the intangible, the *nearly-all*.

⌘

At twenty years old, Nuno thinks a few minutes later, lulled by the faint humming of the stars, a Heaven that exists only in the imagination is no longer enough. We want to find it, real and lasting, here on Earth.

Maybe, by wandering aimlessly, by turning our backs on the crush of humanity, in some far-flung corner of a shadowy land; the place could be invested with the fantasy of a small group of human beings conspiring to achieve *nothingness*. They would wear masks, just for the madness and beauty of doing it. Some of them would carry kaleidoscopes. And then they would march in a glittering procession through the streets.

Nuno knows that there are sources of life on this Earth; emeralds whose gleam can overcome the darkness of struggle, but he despairs at their rarity. He yearns for the magic of the everyday to weave an inhabitable universe, rather than settling for a mirage composed of ephemeral moments amid the mists. He feels, too often, as if his edges are blurred.

Clara keeps her eyes closed, but she is aware. If only this night could last forever. She wonders why, except for the moments spent with Nuno or at her piano, life in Paris bores her so much. Parisians, she thinks, are lacking . . . what? A sense of the tragic.

At the heart of tragedy there is a kind of generous joy, she muses. A sensitivity to invisible beauty; a brave and boundless honesty unattainable by those who are pressed flat against the time they're living in like images in a mirror. Pretense is the price of cowardice; duplicity the rotten fruit plucked by those who never really risk anything.

She knows that the triumph of Love can be felt only by those with the courage to look Devastation square in the eye . . .

Modus operandi

Pa-ri-da-i-za, the website's homepage informs us, is a word taken from the ancient Avestan, and the source of our word *paradise*. In the time of the prophet Zarathustra, alias Zoroaster, it meant "heavenly gardens", the oases built by kings deep in the deserts of Persia.

For many, this Internet Paridaiza, with its unprecedented ability to intoxicate the senses, has become the supreme man-made paradise, a dream and a drug trip combined, a seductive way of letting off stress by becoming virtual, and having encounters and experiences that are surprising and yet—apparently—safe.

This sense-stimulating game, invented at the end of the first decade of the twenty-first century, is a three-dimensional reproduction of Earth; a vast holographic territory referred to by its devotees as *Biearth* to distinguish it from what they now—and not without irony—call *Old Earth*. Cities such as New York, Peking, Moscow, and Paris can be found in Paridaiza, duplicated with unsettling accuracy.

Experts have been insisting for years that the Internet would into a true parallel universe, a new paradigm, once all five senses were brought into play. The Sensorium interface is what makes the real, revolutionary difference between Paridaiza and similar games developed since the early 2000s; it looks like a simple (if large) helmet with built-in headphones, but, thanks to twelve electrodes, it can link a user's brainwaves to his or her computer. Most Internet users have only a very vague idea of how this is done, but it thrills them that the device makes it seem as if they are touching, tasting, and smelling a three-dimensional environment in a way that feels both solid and ethereal, like in a dream.

The faces of the avatars—the humanoid forms assumed by players—are mobile and expressive enough—if a touch waxen—to convince some users that all of these artificial constructs differ profoundly from one another.

Economically speaking, Paridaiza is ruled by the laws of liberalism, if only for the sake of consumer freedom. It boasts a wide range of more or less flourishing businesses, massage parlors, life insurance agencies, bridge clubs, political party headquarters, psychotherapy clinics, water-slide discotheques, musical ski lodges, etc. Biearth's currency, the paridollar, is no more fictional than any other; it can now be converted into any other national value, and is earned and spent in the same way—though perhaps a bit more compulsively. The equivalent of nine hundred and twenty million euros (on average) is spent each day in this virtual world, which already counts nearly one hundred million inhabitants—all of which seems to justify one of its advertising slogans: "Everyone's playing it."

It is sometimes claimed that simulation games make it possible for taboos to be violated and respected at the same time. In Paridaiza, "thought crime" is not only tolerated, but implicitly encouraged. It is not uncommon, for example, for a wife and mother to have a secret, quasi-physical affair with the avatar of a stranger. Or someone might shoot himself in the chest to feel the exquisite agony of intense pain without real consequences, kind of the way you crash heavily to the ground after a dizzying fall in a nightmare, and then wake up unharmed.

Every new registration on Paridaiza allows the user to create a character whose gender and physical appearance they can choose themselves. Often, a single player will have up to three avatars; on Biearth you might come into contact with several characters without ever suspecting that they're all controlled by the same person on the other side of the screen. However, you can only experience sensations through one avatar at a time, while the others are set to Autopilot, a function that allows characters to continue existing when the player is offline.

Godpreview Incorporated, the company behind Paridaiza, doesn't seem to be run by a bunch of utopian dreamers. In the game, power is concentrated in the hands of twenty or thirty thousand characters, called the Ultracollectives. Members of this superior class sit for three-month terms in Parliament, which acts as a sort of combined Ministry of the Interior, High Court, and legislative body where new rules of the game are voted on. The Ultras recruit their members on the basis of paridollars and only after multiple tests that act like hypnotic lures. The qualities they look for are: skill, cunning, and a lack of compassion. Selections are also sometimes made by drawing lots, taking into account the player's reputation—not in terms of any kind of morality, but rather the number of hours he or she has spent playing the game.

The Ultras are surrounded by two million semi-privileged characters called the Collectives. These characters serve as the game's administrative body and are employed by the Vivarium, a vast island deep in the heart of Paridaiza.

Located in the middle of the Biearth-Pacific Ocean, the island is ringed by a thick, humid jungle of red palm trees, full of white-furred monkeys that are sometimes placid, sometimes agitated. As you travel (in a sealed vehicle) toward the center of the Vivarium, you cross through an arid, rocky no man's land in which the air has been made unbreathable to keep away intruders. Eventually you reach an imposing city of interwoven skyways where one similizinc and faux-glass building looms above the rest: the black Absolux tower, a resplendent totem that seems to symbolize an intangible order, a protective supremacy. It is on the uppermost floors of this tower that young Angelot Malaner[x], the avatar of Paridaiza's principal creator, has his headquarters. On Old Earth, Malaner, without whom this world would never have seen the light of day, is idolised by many Internet users. In Paridaiza, his obvious desire for power is a source of concern, among his associates as well as to Parliament.

While it is difficult to become a Vivarist (a resident of the Vivarium), rising to a position of prominence there—a place in the digital sun—is an even more delicate matter. The island's motto is "The Vivarium is the Future of Mankind", and becoming an Ultra, or at least a Collective, is for most players the main objective of the game—because this status, besides banishing any feeling of solitude, also gives you access to the Pleasurium, a supplementary function of the Sensorium, the delights of which are enough to tempt even the most straitlaced soul. For the Pleasurium offers the most sought-after prize among the Vivarists: the ability to feel physical sensation during virtual sex.

BOOK ONE

THE VIVARIUM IS THE FUTURE OF MANKIND

I
DOUBLING

It has already been a year since he saw Clara's long, slim legs for the first time, her ink-black hair and her rounded, full-featured, softly-lined face, as she stood at the coffee machine at the Arsenal library, where she had come to photocopy old sheet music. She wore a miniskirt, and the little voice in Nuno's male brain wolf-whistled.

When he heard her play the piano for the first time a few days later—it was Beethoven's "The Tempest"—she became even more desirable to him, something almost more than human. That stirring, vivacious silhouette—could it be the shape of what we commonly refer to as love?

Clara is stretched out now on the purple duvet, in the half-light of the studio. She has just turned over in her sleep, her body warm and naked on the squeaking sofa-bed. The light of the screen before which Nuno is seated is too dim; he can barely make out her face, fair and shadow-dappled, her hair dark and thick as an Indian girl's. That face, he can tell, has been less amused by his jokes recently, the ones that often used to make her laugh but now fall flat sometimes, like checkers plunked down too hard on a game board. What's bothering her? Why is she showing flashes, now and then, of something that is almost hostility?

It feels—as he wrote in his journal last night—like when she isn't at her piano, the source of all her pride and self-confidence, she seems to float just above the surface of life too much of the time. She watches him sometimes with insomniac intensity; flames dance at the edges of her pupils. She speaks to him as if she's talking to herself, or to some ghost sitting next to the two of them. And then she remembers to smile, and she says:

"It's too bad you're so young."

Is that why she seems to be pulling away from him? The age difference?

Once, when she seemed sad, he gave her a little red music box that played the theme from *Love Story*.

"It's not bad musically," he'd said, almost apologetically. "But I've had this music box since I was twelve."

"It's pretty. Who gave it to you?"

"Does it matter?"

"Maybe."

"You won't believe me."

"Try me."

"Have you heard of Angelot Malaner?"

⌘

Thirty-seven years old and childless, the daughter of an Italian father and a German mother, Clara has long been considered a piano virtuoso. She makes a living giving classical concerts, but for fun she occasionally performs in a jazz trio with the Flipp brothers, Mick (clarinet) and Ludwig (upright bass), who are known as much for their improvisational skills as for their anarchist discourse. Sometimes, in private, she softly sings opera songs like "Casta Diva" from *Norma*, its lyrical melody taking her back to her teenage dreams of being a diva. The rest of Clara's existence was marked by a vague sense of dissatisfaction until she met Nuno, the first man whose innocence seemed capable of bringing the world around her to life.

Nuno's few friends, which are really more like acquaintances, seem baffled by his pursuit of a relationship with a woman seventeen years older than him, a love story already marked by almost as many ferocious arguments as moments of passion. Clara and Nuno themselves have wondered if the gap of a full generation between them might not end up being too wide to cross.

He knows she would like to have his child, and as soon as possible. But he refuses to believe that this "biological and social need" is the missing piece in their mutual puzzle.

More than once in the past she has advised him, without conviction, to end their relationship and go after girls his own age. She thought she could forget him, banish his presence from her mind and her body, insisting to herself that she was still capable of being sensible. But sensibility bored her.

During their periodic breakups, he has tried to go back to more impersonal pleasures; hooking up with semi-strangers, trying to shrug off his emotions and put them on the nightstand the way you take off a watch. Joining a gymnastics club but not attending a single session for fear of feeling ridiculously alone. Going to dance clubs (which only confirm his distaste for conventional entertainments); eating cold pizza in front of the TV; trying to make friends at parties from which his soul shrinks in terror as if they were mass brainwashing sessions. He feels as if he is only pretending to take part in most of the actions that make up daily life for a citizen of the Western world.

And he always ends up back at one of Clara's concerts, plying her afterward with flowers and tears, furtively, like a kidnapper. If he were given to such sentiments, he would write in his private journal that he was not only fascinated by Clara's talent, but caught, like a fish on a hook, in the vast reflection of her shadow, that dark thing whispering that life, like music, is a vast nothingness that fertilises you and devours you at the same time. He would add that he feels duty-bound to stand bodyguard over both the Clara whose moods swing wildly between excess and emptiness, and the Clara whose face sometimes scrunches into a childish pout that causes waves of tenderness to wash through him.

"Pfft, women's moods—they're like a Rorschach test; every man interprets them however he wants to," Clara scoffed one night, her head buried in a sheet of Beethoven's 8th sonata.

⌘

He closes his eyes. Is he becoming a misanthrope already, at his age? His life would be empty without Clara, wouldn't it? The only way to know for sure would be to detach himself from her, for some indefinite period of time. But how can he avoid her without putting too much distance between them?

She's already found *her* refuge: music. It fascinates him, what she does with her instrument. A piano has eighty-eight keys; from them, her slender fingers coax a stream of notes that evokes a parallel world. She sits, her back perfectly straight, on a bench that she prefers to keep very low, and plays with assurance, her gaze often going past the audience to the darkness at the rear of the stage—maybe in an attempt to recapture the solitude of rehearsal, or maybe to commune with what she calls "the Now".

The computer keyboard in front of which Nuno is sitting, frozen, has one hundred and two little white keys whose square surfaces, printed with black letters and numbers, absorb the screen's reflections. Could this keyboard produce music of its own? Create a world?

⌘

He hesitates. He's been more and more tempted over the past several days to explore Paridaiza and its different regions, despite a few misgivings and emerging rumors of addiction—they say that some habitual users, having decided to walk away from this parallel universe, have fallen into apathetic lethargy, and even depression. But so many other players insist that their worries and frustrations have just melted away since they gave themselves up to this unique experience . . .

Maybe this simulation game will be just the thing to soothe his anxiety. Most of the time he feels like he's filled with too much unproductive energy, as if his body is giving off more heat than his mind can convert into action. Once he thought that frequent sex would help to calm this restless effervescence; or that joining the workforce in its daily grind might do the trick, but the more energy he spends in everyday tasks, the more his body burns with a hunger that is seemingly without cause, a boiling that threatens to burst the fragile shell containing it. This feeling is never more acute than when he finds himself at the Arsenal library, where he is interning as an archivist.

Nuno doesn't feel like he's living the unexpected existence of a good improviser. Nor is he attracted by the false successes of "winners". He doesn't normally go out very much, or identify with generally-accepted social motivations: "Have fun by aping the things other people like; make money by following in their tracks; become an artist by filling your Rolodex, bit by bit, with highly impressive addresses; behave like a perpetual boy-king without a kingdom; lie for the sake of vice or resentment . . ."

His gaze comes to rest on the sofa-bed. Clara turns over again in her sleep, one leg poking out from beneath the duvet. She looks so peaceful.

What are you dreaming about?

He sometimes feels as if a sickness has begun to infiltrate the blood of their relationship, though it's just a mild case as yet. This insidious leukaemia has a name: boredom. But he thinks that he's tired of his own discouragement more than anything else, of his lack of faith, of the kind of spectator's inaction that strips us of our determination to apply our creativity to everyday life.

His attention is caught again by the colors dancing in front of him on the glowing computer screen. Sometimes he doesn't feel as if he can live up to Clara's personality. How can he prove himself to himself?

His eyes move from the screen to the palm of his left hand. Those strange, criss-crossing lines.

Clara says he has the hands of a pianist, but what good are those when you don't know anything about music theory?

⌘

Nuno's fingers fly across the keyboard. The die is cast. One credit-card number later, in the nocturnal silence of this January 12th 2012, he has become the $97,354.987^{th}$ inhabitant of Paridaiza. He feels vaguely guilty, but also driven by a strange feeling of necessity.

His first character will share his first name but, going along with a practice that has become trendy recently, he adds a superscript x on the end. Thanks to video-capture of his face in profile and head-on, Nuno^x bears a physical resemblance to Nuno: brown hair; slightly above-average height; cheerful face with angular features; and a gleam of astonishment in the eyes. But, Nuno thinks, the avatar already seems more enthusiastic than its creator, as if its love of life is simpler and more uncomplicated. This is probably due to the fact that, despite recent advances in holographic technology, the avatars still look like wax figures from Madame Tussaud's that can walk and talk.

Still, Nuno reassures himself, the game is bound to be more exciting than fiddling nervously with the old Rubik's Cube he's been able to complete from start to finish since he was a teenager, the habit so ingrained that he can build a house of cards—or worry—at the same time. Now all he has to do is buy a Sensorium helmet tomorrow, and then suggest to Clara that she create a character too.

Will she want to launch into an exploration of Paridaiza with him, or will she say it's too artificial of an escape, and that true adventure happens in real life, when you're least prepared? She might be put off by the technical nature of the game; she is one of those people who, even though they're living in the twenty-first century, use modern devices either reluctantly or as if these things are powered by emotion or will.

A malicious thought occurs to him: maybe, on Paridaiza, they could have a virtual child to pass the time.

It's at this exact moment that her eyes flutter open in the dimness, perhaps just now realizing that Nuno isn't lying beside her anymore. Vaguely guilty, vaguely satisfied, he shuts down the computer, goes to the sofa-bed, slides under the duvet, and curls up against her.

"You okay?" she murmurs drowsily.

If she wakes up all the way, he thinks, she might ask what he's thinking about—that disarming question that even the most intelligent women can't seem to resist; because it is, after all, less a real question than a call to order, or the faint echo of an endless yearning for transparency. What *is* he thinking about, for that matter? The real reason for his interest in Paridaiza, maybe. Jealousy.

He found out a few months ago that Godpreview Incorporated, based in California, is partly headed by the Frenchman Angelot Malaner, twenty-one, heralded as a "computer genius" by the press, whose double in the game is master of the black Absolux tower. Between the ages of eight and twelve, Angelot and Nuno were best friends, growing up just a few doors from one another in a working-class neighborhood in east Paris before losing touch gradually; Angelot's parents had moved the family to London, and then to the United States. Nuno is sure Angelot forgot about him years ago.

On the day he left Paris, Malaner gave him a little red music box that had been a gift from his grandfather. The theme from *Love Story* had become, in a way, a hymn to their friendship. As a child, Angelot had had two passions that seemed diametrically opposed to one another: already endowed with a natural talent for the mysteries of computer technology and electronic circuits, he also collected old music boxes, enchanted by the simplicity of their mechanisms. And he always carried in his pocket the little red box that played that familiar song.

It was the end of the twentieth century. The two little boys loved the idea of chance, and what they called everyday magic. Angelot had noticed that if you rearranged the letters of the French word *image*, you got *magie*—magic—and he often repeated the phrase (where had he discovered it?):

"Without magic, the world is nothing but a graveyard of images."

They would wander the streets of Paris, tossing a coin to determine whether to turn right or left, or whether to speak to the people they passed. They had understood very early that, unless we work to change it, daily life returns to us mostly frozen, monotonous, dead images. Only imagination and faith in the impossible could break through appearances. But Angelot was the one who always took the lead, and Nuno who followed him, starry-eyed and submissive.

Could it be that we keep the same personality all our lives as we have at the age of ten? Nuno feels admiration and envy of his old playmate's success at the same time; Angelot has clearly moved skilfully into the adult world, while he, Nuno, still feels as if he is floating in some adolescent limbo, trying to figure out whether the edifice of his life will be a palace or a nomad's tent.

He remembers the character in that Western film who said to Clint Eastwood: "There are two kinds of people, my friend. Those that come in by the door, and those that come in by the window." Nuno would have liked to add a third type, probably the most common: the ones that never go inside the house at all.

With Paridaiza, Angelot Malaner has helped to build an edifice that might be open to criticism, but is certainly impressive. What he doesn't know is that Nuno and Clara are about to change it. From the inside.

II
Transfer

1
Love Day

Some days, he thinks he would like to take Clara to some desert where neither the past nor the future exists. There would be a piano there, on the rocky horizon. They would feel the intense, painful, joyous sensation of being at the center of the world, recognizable by its shooting stars, and the tails of comets, and the scent of honey and green apples, and the fact that their bodies cast no shadow. She would play Beethoven's *The Tempest*, as if for the first time. All the bad thoughts would crumble to dust on the sand, and . . .

But for several days now, Clara has been distant. She seems dispirited, and keeps saying things that aren't like her, such as:

"I'm too old for you."

What if she's right? Maybe he only fell in love with a mature, artistically accomplished woman because he feels immature, and slightly pointless? Maybe his love for her is a selfish thing.

⌘

February 13th. Today, on my lunch hour, in the basement of the Arsenal, I leafed through dusty volumes about love, and I sneezed. I wondered if maybe the widely-accepted fantasy of exclusive love between two people isn't, as some utopians have suggested, just a derivative of the desire for ownership.

Shouldn't we be capable of loving all humans before we can really love just a single one? Why do most of the people around me seem so pathetic, so sad, and sometimes so contemptible? Is it pretension? I've been asked more than once just who I think I am. But I loathe everything about myself that's mundane and unoriginal, too. It's not just that I'd like to be different from other people. I'd like other people to be different from one another.

In 1688, the theologian Fenelon, who believed that ego was the only thing standing between us and the divine, wrote in a letter to a female mystic, Madame Guyon: "Pure love hates itself; this is why it takes its pleasure from pain." And, further on: "The soul must sacrifice itself without restraint, and without shrinking."

So many thirsting souls associate love with the desire for personal power. Maybe Fenelon was right: to love is to lose sight of oneself.

But I'm afraid of losing myself before I've found myself first.

⌘

Today, February 14th 2012, a lot of online forums are buzzing with the news released at dawn by the people behind Paridaiza: "Love Day". By the end of the year, twenty thousand residents of Biearth-Paris will be chosen at random and teleported to a new city called Agapolis. The event is being described as a "mystical lottery"—an expression, thinks Nuno, that would make Clara smile.

The Internet users hiding behind the chosen avatars will have to have their Sensorium helmets upgraded with a startling feature, already patented under the name of the "Amorium"; if everything goes as planned, any time they are connected they will experience permanent and "unconditional love from their fellow beings", an idea that Nuno finds both attractive and unsettling.

The idea Paridaiza's creators have come up with, touted with unbridled cynicism ("Relax; it's only a game!"), is to test "for the first time, on a large scale and without the possibility of hypocrisy, a program of spiritual love". Less officially, the announcement of Love Day is a way of countering the criticisms levelled at the game by religious associations protesting the lust and depravity encouraged by the Pleasurium.

But can "neuronal love" possibly bear any resemblance to the real love of another person? In 2007, a team of researchers from the Hebrew University of Jerusalem's psychology department believed they had detected the source of altruism and generosity in a gene. Could love for another person really be initiated via neuronal stimulation? That question and a thousand others seem to plague many Internet users on a daily basis, but most of them really want only one thing: to be on the list of the chosen ones. Nuno can understand it, in a way; misanthropy has always been a handicap if you want to have a happy life.

Cleverly, he thinks, Love Day hasn't been planned for next Valentine's Day, but rather for the 21st of December 2012. Many people have pointed out that this is no random selection: a Mayan prophecy (very popular on the Internet) has long been known to predict that this date will mark the beginning of a new era on planet Earth, one that will be more peaceful and honorable, though preceded by years of significant climate imbalance, ridiculous wars, and social unrest.

Probably to avoid a massive overpopulation of Biearth-Paris between now and the final month of 2012 due to an influx of everyone hoping to achieve neuronal love, the lottery announced will only be open to characters whose Internet creators have an address in the real Paris—which Nuno dues. He surprises himself by toying with the idea that he and Clara might be chosen, might start a new life of ecstasy in Agapolis thanks to the Amorium. Who cares what you're drinking, as long as you get drunk?

⌘

Last night, Nuno and Clara attended a recital by the Russian pianist Lugansky at the Theatre des Champs-Elysées. Sitting in their dimly-lit box shared with fiftysomethings dressed in their Sunday best, Clara was moved to tears by a Beethoven sonata. As for Nuno, he found the Russian's playing technically brilliant, but he failed to be transported by it. During the intermission, he couldn't hold back from criticizing the space and the middle-class audience:

". . . and plus the room is too big. You can't even really hear the notes."

It's a clumsy way of telling Clara that he's a bit tone-deaf when it comes to the piano, unless she's the one playing.

After the concert, she refuses to sleep over at his place despite his insistence. "There are other ways to feel emotion besides a roll in the hay," she says, dryly, as she leaves him.

⌘

You can feel lost in a big city, by yourself in your little studio, when you have no desire either to go out—because you don't believe you'll meet anyone you connect with—or to stay alone, wasting your so-called precious youth. Why do I feel so often, at only twenty years old, as if I'm watching my own life from the sidelines?

Do I give myself over to passionate experience often enough? Lose myself in the moment? No matter what I do, disdain and ennui always seem to regain the upper hand.

I would like for my life to be epic, like the lives of the great explorers. My ancestors were Portuguese, after all. How did a country of conquerors, that once reigned over the whole world, become a European afterthought full of depressives? Is it impossible for man to achieve lasting greatness?

I'm going to create a second character in Paridaiza; a more dynamic one than Nuno[x]. I'll call him Orante Magellan[x], in honour of the great Portuguese navigator, the hero, the discoverer of worlds.

Why Orante? Well, partly because Orante Magellan is an anagram of Angelot Malaner!

⌘

He hasn't heard a word from Clara for several days now. Is she even in Paris, or is she performing abroad somewhere? This time, despite missing her deeply at times, Nuno has decided to hold back from calling or texting her. If their relationship needs to end in order for both of them to be better off, it's now or never. In the meantime, to calm himself down when he feels on the verge of losing control, he takes systematic refuge in Paridaiza every evening. During the day he tries, not without difficulty, to concentrate on his internship at the Arsenal library.

He devotes himself to the archives. Every year, hundreds of thousands of pages—often scholarly, sometimes passionately reflective—end up stored as anonymous computer files, the letters of their alphabets transcoded into pairs of 1s and 0s. Nuno has sometimes felt recently as if he, too, is wavering between the urgent desire to become a 1 and the anxious fear of being a 0.

He wants desperately to be self-disciplined, but he is missing some vital component that would allow him to revel in hurting himself. His subconscious seems to be too mischievous to let him lead a model existence. And his shirts are often sloppily ironed.

⌘

Don't listen to recordings of Clara at the piano anymore.
Don't think about Clara's body.

Deep down, did we ever really love each other?

She might have met someone else already, someone who's caressing her even now. It's possible that what I really loved about her was her piano-playing, her art, which set her apart from the masses.

Or maybe it was the curve of her buttocks above those slim thighs?

⌘

Nuno begins to feel sexually deprived, a state that he has always dreaded. Frustration leads to philosophizing. The pages of his journal play host to his slightly overwrought theory that, ever since he was a teenager, he has noticed that his view of the world is never the same *before* and *after* coitus. You could even, he thinks, divide the world—the *masculine* one, at least—into two antithetical moments: the pre-coital phase, and the post-coital phase. Besides, everyone's heard the saying attributed to Aristotle, who wrote: "All animals are sad after sex."

Nuno finds this duality tragic. A lack of sex—everyone knows—can drive a man to acts of desperation, violent encounters, absurd passions, or costly dead-ends. That said, however, it's been two weeks since he last had sex, which puts him in the pre-coital phase—and yet he feels sad.

He takes a sheet of paper and, without thinking about it too much, draws the following:

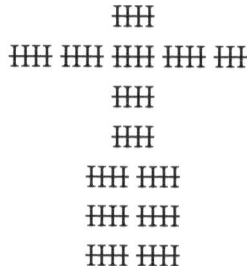

2
Soulmates

Nuno wanted his second avatar to "embody" an anonymous descendant of the great navigator who changed the world five centuries ago with his discovery of the narrow southern passage leading to the ocean he christened "Pacifico"—by following a partly-imaginary map he'd drawn himself to soothe his mad ambition and convince his creditors. Orante Magellan[x] has the sleek body and changeable features—sometimes slack and soft, sometimes sharp and beautiful—of a man still seeking his strait.

Nuno has read somewhere that though most humans pass through the mother's birth canal as they are born, only the most persevering experience a second birth; the only true one, an awakening to oneself and to the world that allows a convergence of love and creativity applied to life. He wonders if Malaner is an awakening.

When you create a character in Paridaiza, it's recommended to sketch out a brief past for that character. So, Orante[x] remembers that his fictional mother used to tell him an alternate version of the Pacific Ocean's birth story:

In the beginning, the Pacific Ocean was a desert of sand . . .

Once upon a time, there was a proud man who, despite the difficulty of walking on the dunes, never fell. Then another man came along who fell often, but was persistent and never gave up. He said that to live was to gain a little ground against death every day.

After a few months of wary attraction, the two men struck up a friendship. Some people who led sedentary lives in the desert's oases wondered which of the men was happier; the one who never fell, or the one who fell often but always got up again? The nomads who travelled in caravans answered that it was too simple of a question—and even a pointless one, truly a question only the lazy would ask: neither of those men was seeking happiness, and neither were they worrying about unhappiness. They were too busy trying to walk against the current, defying the desert of sand.

The one who never fell was not vain about his poise. The one who fell often and always got up never complained. They became more and more devoted to one another, and had renounced all jealousy, it was said.

One day, the two men came across something in the middle of the desert which they took to be a mirage: a very beautiful woman neither old nor young, with raven hair and a pale, luminous face, wearing a crown made of ears of wheat, and with robins fluttering around her.

She came closer. "My name is Clara."

No one knows what happened between the three of them that night, or what was said, but the next day, rather than continuing through the desert, the two men, united forever, had become a lake. They say the woman dived into this lake, and that soon the lake became an ocean.

A calm and powerful ocean, which people called the Pacific.

⌘

Since Paridaiza became almost a daily escape for him, Nuno has felt like there is a thin membrane being woven between his consciousness and reality. The Arsenal library, where he continues to work, with its wood-paneled walls and green-tinted glass windows, looks more like a theatre set to him every day. On the evenings he decides not to go home and ends up by himself in a crowded café, he feels as if he is an extra in a film without a script, directed by someone who is endlessly repeating "Rolling!" in a muffled voice. He feels quite alone.

Curiously, in Biearth-Paris, since the announcement of Love Day, more and more players are claiming to be in search of their Soulmate, an idealistic concept that predates the success of Paridaiza, of course, and has been common since the Western capitals became known as "dens of singledom". But the Soulmate trend has picked up speed over the past few weeks, since the famous Nobel laureate Ludmila Gagarina—who already added fuel to the controversy two years earlier, on Old Earth, with a disturbing experiment involving DNA coding—stated that Internet users who had already found their other halves and were deeply in love before December 21, 2012 would have better luck with the Amorium.

Who is this Gagarina, and what is she out for? Fame? Because of her experiments, which seem to indicate a debatable link between erotic love between two people and love of one's fellow man, Gagarina is considered by some journalists to be a likeable visionary—which doesn't prevent her from being admired, followed, and almost venerated by thousands of simple souls who see nothing wrong with applying the vaguely religious concept of a soul to the universe of Paridaiza.

Many people seem to have no problem admitting what the Sensorium seems to imply: that users would truly be playing around with their own souls.

"Is Clara my Soulmate?" wonders a small voice in Nuno's head, and he feels a tingling in his back and arms, like he wants to laugh but doesn't quite know why.

He still hasn't heard anything from Clara.

Sometimes he wakes up in the middle of the night with his head full of phrases that are troubling and soothing at the same time, such as: "Flee humanity". But through the eyes of Magellan[x], he is gradually coming to see Biearth-Paris differently; the solid stones of the Haussmannian buildings could be worry-absorbing sponges; the streets, promises of epic lives and unexpected affinities. The recreational mechanism of Paridaiza could be watered down into an atmosphere that would be composed not only of hope and oblivion, but which would emanate the spicy perfume of a primordial existence, in which (the same old story, the same desire) people's lives would be insightful and splendid, rather than disunited, seedy, and miserable.

⌘

By April 7th 2012, after several consecutive nights of evolution in the game, Orante Magellanˣ manages to establish a modest part-time Collective position for himself, working mornings (most often on Autopilot) driving a Reminibus, the slim, stealthy airborne shuttles serving Vivarium island. He spends his afternoons as a security guard at the Biearth-Paris Mirror Museum, which competes with the theatres and sex shops lining the Rue de la Gaîté at the foot of the Montparnasse similitower, its baroque premises modeled after the ancient Commedia dell'arte.

Who said that the Vivarium was only a "huge orgiastic brothel"? It is true that since Oranteˣ became a Collective, Nuno has been consoling himself by exploring the delights, via his avatar, of voluptuous pleasures in the company of more or less delectable feminine characters who make him forget the unique taste of Clara's skin, for a while.

Many users who frequently haunt the Pleasurium gradually lose much of their interest in sex on Old Earth, it is said. Most of them don't seem too bothered by this; Paridaiza is now the central place in their inverted existence. But some observers have thought to ask the question: if the Pleasurium gradually reduces users' offline sexual desire, shouldn't the Amorium be expected to have a similar effect on the capacity to love?

Nuno still doesn't know what to think about the possible consequences of December 21st, and the hope that Love Day has aroused. Paridaiza's just a frivolous diversion, right? Why has he become so dependent on it, even to the point of going online—discreetly—at work? Is he just weak, or even a degenerate victim of current trends, or is the path he is following a winding but noble one?

Alone, he sometimes talks—through the mouth of Orante Magellan[x]—to his digital cat, Pacha[x]. The silky-furred animal is, at this very moment, curled up in a ball on the bed in his Vivarium apartment, a wary expression on its face. Magellan[x] asks the cat if it's naïve of him to believe that human society could be enlivened by its profound differences; to hope that our existences could be less formatted, less spiteful, more colorful, more driven by sweet madness and creation. Pacha[x] is a prudent Abyssinian, and does not offer an opinion.

Orante[x] never skips work, even on Autopilot; the Mirror Museum's revenue has doubled recently since Gagarina[x], the avatar of the media-friendly Nobel laureate, gave an interview on one of Paridaiza's news channels, in which she alluded to an obscure Slavic legend: when two soulmates look at themselves together in the same mirror, the mirror will light up.

Certain observers comment ironically—once again—on Gagarina's fanciful personality, but the people behind Godview Incorporated seem thrilled that a scientist, even a mystical one, is giving credit to their game.

They still have no concerns about anything.

Orante[x] strokes Pacha[x]'s head. The animal is programmed to jump up on the radiator at least once per hour, even in the middle of summer, but it is also sensitive to unexpected stimuli; the scrap of nutritional film that its master wads up into a ball and then tosses across the room makes the cat leap after it as if its life depended on it.

On the other side of the screen, Nuno is feeling more and more alone. It's very late. He finally logs off of Paridaiza and takes a thick book with white covers into his study. If nothing happens over the next few days to give a new direction to his existence, he'll have no other option but to memorize these lines from the philosopher Heidegger: "Equivocation, idiosyncrasy, appearance, amorality—all have become stronger in these times. Have we become so insignificant that we need a role to play? . . . Is this because, apart from everything else, we are being confronted with *indifference*, the reasons for which we do not understand?" He rereads these abstruse words several times in the nocturnal silence; they lodge like incandescent stones deep in his gut.

He's sure of one thing: despite Paridaiza, he is bored without Clara and the Arsenal archives. Boredom, he thinks, is what happens when the soul, discouraged by unfulfilled possibilities and slowed by indecision, falls into the depths of emptiness—at the bottom of which are even more unfulfilled possibilities, which is extremely boring, etc.

Unless boredom—that numbness with its flavor of dust—is caused by not seeing that *we are* the depths, and the unfulfilled possibilities?

He wonders, finally, if what he's thinking of as boredom isn't really just another new role: the mask of a person paying his debt to the spirit of seriousness, out of a lack of courage to own joy, or fear of making himself vulnerable by throwing himself wholeheartedly and happily into new risk?

What he doesn't know is that Clara has not really pulled away.

She hasn't stopped caring.

True, she tried briefly to forget him by playing several weeks of concerts abroad, but it didn't work. Now she is trying to think of the best way to build a lasting relationship with Nuno. And, despite a few misgivings, she has just signed up—without telling him—for the simulation game that she knows has become the retreat and refuge, sanctuary and shelter, hideaway and hermitage of the man she loves.

3
Clara^x

A springtime without love is a sorrowful thing. People claim that, in the twenty-first century, we recover from romantic disappointments more quickly, but Nuno hasn't managed to get over Clara yet. Sometimes at dawn he wakes up with a jolt, filled with desire so immense, so obvious, so intense, that it feels as if the origins of the universe are surging through him. So he gets up, drinks a glass of cold milk, and feels a little more calm. *Be patient*, a voice inside him murmurs. *Trust in time.*

For several days now, when he's asleep, he's been having the most vivid recurring dreams, which take place in a forest that resembles the tropical jungles ringing the island of Vivarium. In one, a certain Clara^x, an iridescent apparition that looks just like the real Clara, comes toward him smiling, dressed in a silky violet dress, robins fluttering around her head. The couple walks hand in hand among the palm trees, drawing hoots from the white monkeys hanging in the vines overhead.

There is also this strange scene: they are dancing in the middle of a clearing to the amplified strains of a red music box Nuno has given Clara, and which Angelot gave him. They whirl until they collapse, breathless. They gaze at the beauty of nature around them, overjoyed, and make love on the rich loam.

Until now, Nuno's rationalist Western education has led Nuno to consider dreams an insignificant phenomenon, pleasant but without any real usefulness except as a sort of biological exhaust valve enabling people to close out their lives only half-crazy. As a teenager he possessed a dream-key, an old Freud-inspired dictionary of symbols bought in a second-hand shop for the price of two *pains aux raisins*.

Taking a bath with a dolphin means you want to make love and also to become more spiritually enlightened.

Carrying an umbrella means you're protecting yourself from sadness, and you also want to make love, and to become more spiritually enlightened.

Biting into a slice of chocolate cake means an incredible financial opportunity is coming your way, or a fruitful encounter, and also that you want to make love and become more spiritually enlightened.

He quickly understood that even if you manage to figure out the meaning of a dream, it's rare to feel that sensation of absolute clarity confirming the interpretation. There are always a hundred other possible explanations. Like water or sand, dreams slip through your fingers, leaving nothing in your hand but a few glittering traces, sometimes a painful emptiness, and the desire to make love and become more spiritually enlightened.

He doesn't need a dream-key to tell him that he still loves her, but he can never seem to summon up the resolve to try and get her back. Maybe they need this vague silence that tries each day to dry up the well of their passion. And after all, he tells himself not un-hypocritically, if Clara only has two or three years left to become pregnant, biologically speaking, it's better for her to be free to find someone older, someone more responsible. Someone with the desire to be a father and a healthy stock portfolio. There were plenty of other men interested in her during their relationship, often five or six years older than her.

Isn't the fact that she vanished from his life proof that she wants to move on? To turn a new page?

Except that, when you turn the page of a book, it's because you're curious to see what comes next.

⌘

It's the morning of May 25, 2012, according to Nuno's diary. His separation from Clara has lasted more than three months. If someone had told him three weeks ago that not a word, not a message, not a sign would pass between them for all that time, he wouldn't have believed such an ordeal possible. It's 9:30 in the morning. He turns on the espresso machine at the Arsenal library. It was here that she burst suddenly into his life more than a year ago, exquisite, with her short skirts and her endless pages of sheet music.

That's all over now, he thinks, fatalistically. All the pages have been turned. The story ends here. It was a beautiful one. Pulsing with life.

Goodbye, Clara; I love you. Be happy. We could have stayed friends . . .

Behind him, an impatient fellow archivist suggests that, if he's having trouble deciding between tea and coffee, he can always have both. The remark seems to light an unexpected spark in his mind; a few minutes later he is sending a speedily-typed e-mail to Clara from his desk, signed *Magellan*ˣ, *watchman, Mirror Museum of Paris-Paridaiza*. The message consists solely of an extract from Goethe's *Faust*, the original 1828 edition of which, translated by Nerval, is held by the Arsenal:

"What a vision! What a celestial image this magic mirror doth enshrine! The very loveliest image of a woman! Is it possible woman can be so lovely?"

It is lyrical, but a week goes by and Clara doesn't respond.

⌘

Nuno buries himself in the shifting sands of moroseness and disenchantment. He bites his nails, takes refuge in Paridaiza until ungodly hours, smokes cigarillos that make him cough and feel nauseated, chews lemon-flavored gum until it tastes like detergent.

In Biearth-Paris, the quest for symbiotic love legitimized by the ramblings of Ludmila Gagarina and further inflamed by the prospect of the Amorium gives a semblance of human warmth to certain streets, where

Agape and Eros are casually blended. Some bars even come close to brimming over with a brief illusion of joy. Two thousand years after the deaths of Ovid and Christ, the term *soulmate* has been turned into a catchy buzzword; the desire for twinship is flourishing from Saint-German to Barbès, from Bercy to the gates of Versailles—all of these neighborhoods reproduced to perfection, including the dirt, the slight haze of pollution, and the weathered stone. It must be said that most of the virtual residents have few personal ideals, if any; the promises of the Amorium, the mysteries of the Vivarium, and the delights of the Pleasurium serve as their perfect Utopia.

⌘

I think there is a lot of hypocrisy in this "soulmate" fad. Internet users these days only care about surface aesthetics. In Paridaiza like anywhere else, women and men prefer young avatars with symmetrical features. There's a reason so few characters are unattractive, obese, or nondescript.

In his own time, a certain Jesus suggested that existence would be more peaceful if the world's population was kinder and less dishonest. Others, all others, should be as important (or more so) than oneself. But humans seem to prefer the seemingly less effortful idea of an emotional relationship reduced to a single couple, even though it's the cause of so much disappointment.

To those female players inviting me out for a drink, I confess that I am sensitive to the needs of this fleshly envelope—but also to the words inside it. Recently, though, that inner message has seemed repetitive and tedious to me: "What if we join together to forget our mediocrity and form a weapon against the rest of the world?"

Clara is an extraordinary woman. I lost her because I was superficial . . .

⌘

A few days later, Orante Magellan[x] makes his way through the Mirror Museum's small rooms, dim and ornate as boudoirs. Between the gleaming reflections of the spherical, concave, or convex surfaces with their silver and gold gilt frames, sometimes set with precious stones, he finds himself lazily stroking the crimson velvet walls, warm as internal organs.

He stops in front of an eighteenth-century Venetian mirror decorated with jade and ivory, on whose pedestal is engraved another Goethe quote: "No doubt you can see the truth only as my mirror shows it in its purity."

Just after 5:30, a feminine voice murmurs directly into his left ear:

"I wanted to see where you work . . ."

Is Nuno hallucinating? Is he really seeing, through the eyes of Orante[x], the Clara[x] from his dreams, standing beside him in the mirror, which seems lit from within?

Anyone clapping a set of sensors on Nuno's head at moment would be witness to a storm of miniature short-circuits, but the agitation of his brain is a pale reflection of the simple ecstasy flooding through his veins.

Love, he thinks, watching Clara[x] walk from mirror to mirror—she is almost frolicking now, as if she has been set free from something—alongside a dozen reflected echoes of herself, love is nothing but an increase of serotonin; it's an effervescence that pops the cork plugging the skull, it's the certainty that parallel universes exist; it's four hands gliding side by side across the keyboard of a piano, bodies consuming each other and giving birth to one another at the same instant; tapping the void to drink the sap of our joys; laughing like a child sitting astride a geyser; sleeping in a tent in the middle of a palace, in a prince's bed in the heart of a luxuriant jungle!

Clara[x] whispers in his ear:

"*Monsieur* Magellan[x], did you know there is a kind of butterfly called an *éphémère*, whose reflection can hardly be seen in a mirror? Would you please tell your friend Nuno[x] that I would like to invite him to dinner tomorrow night, very near here, at the top of the Montparnasse similitower. Nine o'clock sharp."

With a floating movement, she slips into the Crystal Mirror Room, toward the exit. On the other side of the screen, Nuno suddenly feels the need for a cup of coffee. *And* a cup of tea. Clara is back!

But she has come wearing a mask.

III

Immersion

1
The antisocials

Nuno[x] looks around, surprised: the top floor of the
Biearth-Montparnasse tower looks like an old-fashioned London club tonight, with its woodwork and
Chesterfield sofas and its paintings of dogs in suits
playing billiards and smoking pipes. Picture windows
overlook Paridaiza-Paris, which stretches away in glittering fractals. A dozen small tables "realize" the restaurant space, with waitresses dressed in purple silk gliding
among them.

When a couple who are broken up but still in love
find themselves face to face at a table, each of them
expects to express out loud all the thoughts, poetic
or defeatist, that have crossed their minds during the
separation. But it often happens that the serious words
refuse to come, that they are held back by fear and, out
of shyness, perhaps, replaced with lightness. And is the
ease with which Clara and Nuno joke with one another
also due to the fact that they are each hiding behind a
mask?

Nuno[x] seems more and more startled; he finds
Clara[x] different, more playful, than the real Clara. She

has obviously spent the last several weeks exploring Paridaiza, and not without curiosity. She seems to have something in mind.

"Let's forget our disagreements," she says, taking a sip from her third glass of similichampagne. "You're young; you want to have fun, and I want to have fun with you. But not small-time fun. Not without a purpose."

"I don't know what I want anymore."

"You're going round in circles."

"What do you mean about wanting to have fun with a purpose?"

"I mean," she answers, her tone conspiratorial, "that we could try to change things in Paridaiza. Make the game less predictable, not just for us, but for others too. I want to introduce you to Ludwig[x] and Mick[x]. They're avatars of the Flipp brothers, the jazz musicians you've seen me play with. They've got some interesting ideas about how we might introduce a grain of sand into this huge mechanism."

"Why are you doing this?"

"Maybe because I'm bored without you. Maybe because this world keeps getting more and more brainwashed and apathetic, and I can't take it anymore."

⌘

Not so very long ago, on Old Earth, this early in the morning, it was possible to breathe in an intoxicating Northern wind, laden with the scents of pine and the future. Here, it smells more like ginger and musk. It's dawn on June 8, 2012. The sound of a violent collision just split the air outside, like some immense metal trunk being wrenched open, and there was a crash, like things breaking.

From the balcony of his solitary room, in which certain objects—a lamp, a chair, the nightstand, a winking Buddha statuette—gleam like zinc, Orante Magellan[x] can't see anything out of the ordinary, except a few passers-by who have started walking a bit faster. Yet he senses that something has shifted in the artificial calm that is supposed to reign on the Vivarium.

In the kitchen, the large red numbers on the digital clock read 6:30. Every time he teleports onto the island, it takes him a few minutes to get into character. The first thing he does is feed Pacha[x], who bounds into the kitchen emitting sharp little meows accompanied by loud purring.

Orante[x] takes a few steps and opens the similisteel door of his apartment. He looks under the doormat; he forgot to renew his subscription, so he'll have to go out and buy a copy of today's *Happenings*. Sometimes, while he's reading the paper, he allows himself a single Krystos, a brand of tobacco-free cigarillo normally reserved for the elite. He knows no one will call him on the carpet for it; Magellan[x] the Reminibus driver is listed as a relatively promising member of the Collective, unlike the Antisocials.

The ones the authorities call the Antisocials have been causing trouble on the otherwise thriving island for five or six weeks now. The group is made up of characters who have managed to secure places on Vivarium

Island, but seem to have reacted abnormally to the use of the Pleasurium. In only a few days they have been overtaken by a sort of apathy, similar to the effects of the obsolete drug opium. They have retreated gradually into relative solitude, a state that goes against the core principles of Paridaiza.

After debating the subject, however, Parliament has chosen not to banish them; it's undeniable that the Collectives' happiness has actually been accentuated in a way by the presence of these unfortunate, and apparently inoffensive, elements. It's as if a social micro-class is gradually emerging on the island, whose only function is to comfort the dominant members of society in the knowledge that they alone are receiving privileges that they have earned through innate predisposition. Not everyone is entitled to pleasure.

Unlike the Antisocials, the Ultracollectives never spend a single minute alone. They live in Transparency and are whip-slender, their skin slightly translucent. The Collectives, who are slightly heavier, still feel the need for solitude, though only rarely. But any Vivarist who spends more than four hours a week alone is now suspected of being an Antisocial, a rule recently proposed to Parliament by Malaner[x] in person.

Charming and dark-haired, with the allure of a sober dandy, Malaner[x] is reputed to have an astonishingly steady character for a young man barely over twenty. The double of the most famous member of the Godpreview Inc. board of directors, he is (of course) an Ultracollective, and one of the most influential ones at that. He administers Absolux, the company responsible for ensuring the smooth internal operation of the Sensorium, not to mention the Pleasurium, with a great deal of skill.

Angelot Malaner[x] is one of those rare people whose intuition is precociously unerring. He almost never doubts himself, and his aim is usually true. But what makes him most attractive, perhaps, is that beneath his ambition and his thirst for power there still lies a certain idealism of the kind which, with time, might kindle a kind of altruistic sensitivity in his soul—or mutate into blind fanaticism.

⌘

The two Vivaguards standing watch tonight at the foggy entrance of the Vivarium shine their flashlight-beams into the eyes of the driver, a very young man with dyed reddish hair. He smiles at them.

The green truck that has just pulled up at the southern security gate of Paridaiza's capital is not a large one, but its cabin possesses the required airtight seals and pressurization equipment without which no vehicle can cross the no man's land surrounding the Vivarium. The red-haired young man plunges his hand into a bag of salt-and-vinegar potato chips, waiting for authorization to pass into the decontamination chamber and then vanish into the city streets.

As expected, the guards ask him what he is transporting. And, as planned, he rattles off a list of objects intended for the Humanist Museum, the space dedicated to the history of Old Earth which is housed on the first three floors of the Absolux Tower. He shows them his authorization form, a perfect fake which, though it doesn't betray him, does little to satisfy the officers' curiosity.

When he opens the truck's cargo door, their flashlights illuminate a dusty collection of objects without much apparent value: a wooden writing desk with rococo drawers, a green oil lamp bearing the stamp *made in India*, a small metal bed, a few used party games including *Risk* in battered cardboard boxes, a poster print of Van Gogh's *Église d'Auvers-sur-Oise*, a net bag of multicolored marbles, and a few other items vaguely reminiscent of a child's bedroom from the last third of the twentieth century.

Threading their way through the jumble of odds and ends, the two soldiers conduct their inspection carefully. After a moment, they pick out a palm-sized red box equipped with a tiny crank-handle. One of the men turns the handle, and the music box emits its crystalline sound. The other guard laughs.

"It's the anthem of the Pleasurium!"

The young driver waits calmly for the guard to stop smiling and then remarks casually, rummaging in his bag of chips: "In the late twentieth century, most people just called it the theme from *Love Story*."

2
The Great Night

Tonight, in his room, Nuno doesn't turn on his computer. The sensation of emptiness is gone, but now he feels hampered somehow. Shackled. He raises a glass of iced vodka to his lips, caresses the surface of his coffee table, looks at his sofa-bed and then out the window at the city lights; ordinary, constant, somnolent. A great capital of the Western world.

He flips through his private diary, whose leather cover he loves to touch. The alcohol stirs him. He strokes himself distractedly through his trousers, then pulls himself together. Why is Clara still refusing to see him outside of the game?

⌘

On this morning of July 14, 2012, a little before seven-thirty in the morning, a bizarre attack occurred in an affluent part of Biearth-Paris, more precisely in the Place Victor-Hugo, not far from the Arc de Triomphe. The bomb, an obviously homemade one, did nothing more than frighten a relatively old couple (two of the very few avatars in Paridaiza whose faces are slightly lined) and their toy poodle, which was wearing a little quilted pink coat with removable hood. Responsibility for the explosion has just been claimed, in a message sent to the Vivarium Parliament, by a group calling itself the "Hazardous Intraterrestrials!", which has again ended its missive with the cryptic phrase, "The world is your improvisation."

The method of the group the press is calling HI! has, for several weeks now, consisted of setting off explosives in places that appear to lack any political relevance. It seems rather sloppy, even absurd; what can be the point of scaring middle-class urbanites dressed in CyberChanel, even if they do represent an undeserving elite? Unless these clumsy explosions are part of a more ambitious plan . . . ?

⌘

Today, at the Arsenal, I stumbled across a book published after the Second World War: The Rape of the Mind, *written by a brainwashing specialist called Joost Meerloo.*

Deep within each human lie two contrary drives: the desire to become him- or herself, and the desire to no longer be anything at all. We have the subconscious wish to be swallowed up and digested by a society that we wrongly identify as being vitally powerful. Under ideal circumstances, the need for anonymity and the need for self-affirmation balance each other out. But in periods of stress, governed by irrational fear and frustration, the unconscious desire to give way, to stop existing, to be as if dead, can become irresistible, though it is sometimes masked by an urge for exhibitionist success, according to the star system *model.*

Sometimes I feel old and weary before my time, like atoms of fatigue are eating away at my brain. In these moments I wish so much that I could wake up, but sometimes I feel like all my efforts to be sharp and alert are for nothing, and it seems like the best thing might be for me just to disappear, to give myself up to the Nothingness. We can't all become famous, like Malaner. And then I smoke cigarettes, which makes me even more exhausted.

It's strange; Clara seems more interested in Paridaiza than I am. Now she's saying we have to keep Love Day from happening, that the Amorium would be an abomination.

The date December 21, 2012 was sacred to the Mayans. On that day, for the first time on Earth in twenty-six thousand years, the sun will appear at the intersection of the Milky Way and the ecliptic plane, that great circle travelled by the yellow star as seen from our planet. A few seconds before sunset, expected to occur at 4:56 pm, Venus will disappear beneath the western horizon as the Pleiades rise in the east. This "cosmic cross" will be a strait leading to a more peaceful era, one in which humans will cease to be mere spectators of their own destiny and become lucid creators.

⌘

The next morning Orante^x sits at the zinc table in his kitchen, the walls of which are hung with photos of Pacific islands. At his feet, Pacha^x regurgitates a small and very realistic puddle of vomit. According to the newspaper, another Reminibus crashed yesterday, this time into the wall of a building not far from the Absolux tower. Sixty-seven characters were killed instantly in the accident. The similiblood and similiguts are almost as impressive and sticky as the real thing.

Orante[x] knows it is virtually impossible to lose control of one of those machines. To him, it's obvious that if a Reminibus veers off its trajectory, it can be due only to an intentional action by the driver, or a breach of the guidance system.

Opposite this story, on the same double-page, is the announcement of an important new Paridaizan law, much less playful than the ones that came before it. In the article, Godpreview states that an antiviral measure will be implemented within the next few days, intended to prevent breaches, whether they are caused by the Antisocials or not. Dubbed *The Great Night*, the principle of the new legislation is as simple as it is spectacular: any character displaying suspicious behavior will see its world shrink like Balzac's magic skin, slowly overtaken by nothingness, a black night engulfing everything until every bit of explorable territory vanishes, followed by the avatar itself.

This antivirus will affect only characters suspected of harboring seditious designs; The Great Night will remain invisible to the majority of players, those who obey the rules of the game, are fascinated by sensitive holograms, adore the thrill of competition, or are lured by the charms of the Pleasurium.

Orante[x] keeps reading while he shaves in front of the bathroom mirror, letting a few blobs of simil-foam drop onto the newspaper, while Pacha[x] watches him with an idiotic expression of feline curiosity.

On the other side of the mirror, Nuno wonders if he shouldn't secretly hope for The Great Night to swallow up his doubles. He's beginning to think he can no longer definitively quit Paridaiza of his own free will.

In an interview published in the Arts & Culture section of the same paper, the ubiquitous Malaner[x] announces the new Absolux slogan: "The Pleasurium is the resort of Supermen." The Antisocials have been circulating a rumor for a couple of weeks now that the waves emitted by the Pleasurium can be used for purposes other than the purely orgasmic. It is possible, apparently, to introduce subliminal suggestions, advertising-based or otherwise, at the moment the erotic tension reaches its peak. For now, most Collectives are treating the idea as a joke, and Nuno would rather not think about it; the Pleasurium is already an effective enough tool for population control, in his opinion.

For the president of Absolux to make a subtle reference to the motto of the Vivarium—"The Vivarium is the Future of Mankind"—is possibly his way of provoking his associates, of declaring implicitly: *The real power lies with me.* But it could also be a warning from Malaner[x] to the most rebellious Antisocials, who are rumored to be forming a small resistance group meeting somewhere in the underground tunnels beneath the city: *If you continue to challenge the Sensorium, you'll have to answer to me, and we'll see who comes out the winner.*

But do these rebels really exist, or have they simply been invented by Paridaiza's programmers?

Nervous, Orante[x] swallows a dose of coffee-flavored serotonic and keeps reading. In an hour he'll be at the controls of a MIR-33 Reminibus, a new model, yellow and ovoid. Its aerial route covers the southern zone of a city of clean, towering buildings, interlacing covered walkways from one building to another, translucent glass whose glinting colors change with the sunlight, rounded tubular conduits reminiscent of blood vessels and, on the roofs and even on the ground, a profusion of domes vaguely evocative of female breasts, across the smooth domes of which stream in bright script the words of a phrase as repetitive as a heartbeat: "The Pleasurium is the Resort of Supermen."

⌘

Shortly before midnight, in Biearth-Paris, Nuno[x] and Clara[x] enter a modern apartment eighty meters square, emptied of its furniture and packed with around fifty characters, a few of whom dance nonchalantly. Some of them are smiling; others look faintly arrogant. This is no agitators' party.

Behind the eyes of his double, Nuno has the impression that most of the guests are displaying a sort of forced casualness, maybe because for the most world-weary of them, the true catastrophe wouldn't be getting absorbed by The Great Night, but rather losing their jaunty composure. It might also be true that this sense of placidity is a digital effect with nothing real behind it, like in photoshopped pictures of fashion models.

Nuno[x] silently observes the array of waxy faces, while Clara[x], laughing in the kitchen, seems more at ease in this ethereal social comedy. The apparent diversity of the faces, he thinks, is a monotonous chant, as if everything is coated with a plastic film. Is it possible that some have resigned themselves to waiting for the Love Day lottery the way people used to wait, not so long ago, for the Olympic Games, or the World Cup?

Beneath the syncopated hum of conversation he can just make out *Spirits in a Material World*, an old song by a British rock group from the 1970s, The Police. Following the rhythm of the base toward a set of speakers, Nuno[x] closes his eyes. He feels caught between the desire to flee and the temptation of frivolity.

He imagines himself driving alone on a wooded back road, leaving the capital, tearing space as if it were tracing paper, electric chords vibrating in arpeggio throughout the car. Among the endless slim trunks of the trees here in the forest of Compiègne, drawers open and close, releasing flocks of robins. Nuno wonders, once again, where his love for Clara has gone.

It has been several months now since they saw each other in flesh and bone. It seems to him that the transposition of their relationship to Paridaiza, rather than bringing them closer, has made the bond between them more inconsistent. Sometimes the past feels as false as

71

a simulation game. The days when they attended piano recitals together seem to belong to the realm of illusion. In his head, dreams, virtuality, and reality have blurred together for some time now into a single hypnotic dance. It's as if classical logic is gradually losing all meaning.

Last night he dreamed that his eyebrows had grown thicker and seemed almost to open up, like lips. A sign, perhaps, of trouble ahead . . .

IV
Permeation

1
The plot

On the morning of August 2nd, emerging from his
building and turning left two blocks down, Orante
Magellanx realizes what caused the deafening noise
that woke him up this morning. Another Reminibus
has crashed at the foot of one of the breast-like domes.
Aerial ambulances have taken away the bodies, and
nothing remains now but the smoking carcass of the
aircraft, watched over by two stone-faced Vivaguards.
With a brusque motion of one hand, in which each
clutches a phosphorescent blue tube like a relay baton
no one wants to take, the guards instruct the gathering
crowd to disperse.

Orantex looks away from the mass of crushed metal,
which has been rapidly cleaned of any trace of blood
or flesh. Again, this can't be an accident. But a sort of
law of silence reigns within his profession; officially,
these incidents are due to technical malfunction. The
rare journalistic comments that have been made re-
garding the crashes have generally blamed them on
overly-abbreviated periods of road-testing for the later
models. New information comes out only sporadically;

Happenings has reported on only three Reminibus crashes, a mere twenty percent of the actual number.

He catches the eyes of several curious bystanders, obvious Antisocials, judging by their colorful clothing—apparently an inverse reflection of their moroseness, or maybe a sign that they aren't in such a bad state after all, deep down. Generally speaking, very few Collectives tend to loiter on the sidewalks, and when they do it's only in groups, usually at night. And even then they're in homogenous clusters, often dressed in white to imitate the Ultras, walking back along the main streets after dinner, frequently headed for a nearby gym. Electrosquash has become the trendy sport lately; it is, as its name indicates, a variant of squash played in teams of four on courts half the normal size. Upon contact with an avatar's body, the ball imparts an electric shock considered harmless to the player.

Orante[x] always goes to the Reminibus depot in the southern part of the city on foot. He wonders if the glances he receives from some other pedestrians—fixed and insistent—might be intended to convey a sense of unity, but the real explanation, he thinks, is less optimistic. The solitude, the marginalization, have probably become oppressive even for those who continue to seek it out. Their eyes seek vague refuge in the pupils of others, betraying the subconscious need for confirmation of their own existence. Heaving a deep sigh, Magellan[x] turns down the street on which the Reminibus depot stands.

Suddenly, a voice with an Eastern accent murmurs in his left ear:

"We may not be able to prevent the birds of sadness from fluttering above our heads, but we can keep them from building their nests in our hair."

He stops. Next to him is a bright-eyed young Asian woman with white-blonde hair and a large, solid body. She slows down, as if trying to find her way, and darts a smile at him. He is surprised to feel an immediate faint stirring of desire. The skin of her face is translucent, suggesting that she has undergone a Transparency treatment very recently, which for the Collectives is a rare luxury. She glances around before speaking to him again:

"The birds of sadness, Orante Magellan[x]. It's a Chinese proverb."

Her eyebrows knit slightly. Her expression tenses. Without waiting for a response, she adds:

"You usually get off work at 1:00 in the afternoon. I'll meet you here in three days, at 1:30. Call me Kim[z]."

The young woman hurries off before he can answer, pulling a small mobile phone from her pocket. She can't be more than a few inches over five feet tall, but weighs around a hundred and eighty pounds. Orante[x] finds her attractive, different; most players choose avatars with angular, mathematically symmetrical faces, rail-thin bodies, and heights a good deal above average.

Troubled, Nuno logs off, leaving his double to continue its day on Autopilot. Has he crossed paths with an honest-to-goodness rebel?

⌘

The master of the Absolux tower has left his offices to return to his enormous penthouse with its minimalist décor by Korga[x], the famous interior microdesigner. Now he dips his hand into the hot water of the vast bathtub in which his similibody is currently immersed, then lifts it majestically, observing the ultra-realistic streaming of the soapy liquid between his fingers. His smile is serene. It is almost 1:30 pm in the Vivarium. The heart of Biearth is beating at full capacity.

How has a place that doesn't actually exist anywhere managed to become a focal point for the desires and ambitions of so many Earth-dwellers? Because they were tired of their lives, Malaner repeats to himself behind his double. The choices of most humans are still determined mostly by what they are running from, rather than their beliefs. In political discussions (which hardly ever take place in the Vivarium anymore except as a joke), he tends to compare Old Earth to a bowl of water:

"Pour in a few drops of wine. Stir. The water will remain clear. Courage and daring have been diluted among the masses in the same way."

Angelot Malaner[x] feels courageous. But he also likes rose petals in his bathwater. He likes the traditional massages provided by Kim[x], who left half an hour ago. His skin is still tingling from its contact with her hands. Nothing beats the caress of her similifingers. Something indefinable, soothing, emanates from that young woman. It's not her platinum hair or the curves of her body, which, anyway, he has always been careful never to touch; Malaner[x] never feels sexually frustrated.

He invented the machine that suppresses that sort of thing.

Built-in speakers in the ceiling emit the Eastern sounds of a Russian goudok accompanied by robin-song. In this immense bathroom with its wooden floors, illuminated only by the shadowy flickering of candlelight, he shivers, and lets out a relaxed laugh. On the other side of the mirror, Malaner remembers knowing with certainty, one day in 2006, that a cycle of human history was well and truly ending. On his way through Paris he had visited the Palais de Tokyo, then devoted to modern art, and had stood frozen in front of an enormous installation by an artist from North Africa: a human skeleton seventeen meters long, floating on its stomach like a dinosaur.

Now he instructs his double to stand up in the tub. The last few years of the old world, according to Malaner, have ended up as a kind of nameless ideological slop, a sort of aimless freewheeling trajectory, stupid and violent, crammed with the most inconsistent and incompatible values. Angelot[x] shakes his head, slips on a robe, leaves the bathroom, and walks to the picture window overlooking the center of the Vivarium.

His gaze travels over the nearest buildings. This city, he thinks triumphantly, is a well-tuned instrument; a music box whose perpetual state of bliss is owed largely to him. How can his associates understand that the Sensorium is only the first stone in his grand vision?

All told, there are few people, even among his closest colleagues at Godpreview, who would think that he, one of the richest young men on Vivarium, also considers himself one of the most idealistic. From among the many possibilities opened up by the success of Paridaiza, he has chosen one mission: to encourage, by any means possible, the emergence of a new kind of humanity, one finally liberated from its fears, from the endless plagues of frustration, resentment, and gloomy fatalism. The reason Absolux continues to release ever more high-performing versions of the Pleasurium is his awareness that, in order to evolve, our gray matter needs sweet treats as well. Brains dulled by decades of nihilism don't come alive for anything anymore except the prospect of pleasure, but in Malaner's eyes, these are simply the first steps to freedom. As long as humanity is weighed down by frustration and petty desire, it will never experience anything new.

Turning collective love into something inevitable, turning it into instinct—like in some insects—via the Amorium, is the good news to come. At least, that's what he wants to think. The Love Day experiment should give a clearer sense of things.

But for that to happen, the Amorium needs to function properly . . .

He turns away from the window, suddenly overcome with a sensation of vertigo. He has tried his hardest not to worry, but his pleasure has been touched with bitterness ever since his Godpreview colleagues, against his wishes and due to pressure from shareholders, announced the date of Love Day. December 21, 2012 is too soon. The latest tests of the Amorium have done little to reassure him.

80

Better to be cautious when it comes to both the Ultras and the media, which is why he has taken so many trips to Biearth-Paris, far from the noise and furor. He runs a harmless workshop there that produces music boxes in luxury similiwoods, a hobby he officially refers to as "returning to his roots" and which, to be honest, takes him back to his childhood.

A week ago, he allowed himself to tell a journalist about one day in particular that he would never forget, the day he turned twelve. He had sat on the roof of a truck parked in the Bois de Vincennes, on the shore of the Lac des Minimes, with a very close friend his own age, a boy called Nuno. They had played together with a little red music box Malaner's grandfather had given him. Gazing out at the still waters of the lake, little Angelot had declared solemnly:

"I will never renounce my pride."

Eleven years have passed since then. It was partly in remembrance of that moment that Malaner wanted the anthem of the Pleasurium to be an arrangement of the theme from *Love Story*. But it was ironic, too, of course . . .

The big apartment in Absolux tower is perfectly silent. It's almost two o'clock. Malaner[x] visibly doesn't want to return to work; he has just sat down at a grand piano made by a company in Estonia[x]. He presses a button beneath the keyboard and the instrument begins playing by itself, the keys sinking one after another as if touched by a ghost. *Come to think of it*, he muses, *whatever happened to Nuno?*

⌘

With Kim[x] leading the way, Magellan[x] enters for the first time one of the Vivarium's underground tunnels. Urban legend has always claimed their existence, but Nuno always believed this was propaganda aimed at marginalizing the Antisocials. Yet, a few minutes ago, the young Asian woman compelled his double to go into the cellar of a speakeasy and, behind the bottles, prodded him into a passage dug into the similirock.

"You're inside the Labyrinth," Kim[x] reveals, nodding at the glistening walls, from which particles of damp clay trickle here and there, and which are studded with pointed protrusions of what appears to be granite and gypsum. "Sorry to be so forceful with you," she continues, her voice hardening a bit, "but it's obvious that you've already seen too much, and if you don't cooperate, the Vivarium will have to add another suicide to the tally."

He decides not to answer and keeps walking. For the rebel Antisocials to claim responsibility for the wave of suicides currently striking the island, particularly among Reminibus pilots, is probably an exaggeration. At least, he hopes so. An uncertain voice in his head murmurs that all of this is only a dream. The tunnel widens.

They come to a large, dimly-lit cave decorated with the signs of the Zodiac, where a dozen characters await them dressed in flamboyant clothing reminiscent of a circus troupe. Some of them sit on wooden stools around a heap of objects and furniture that awaken a clear memory in him.

"Believe in astrology, do you?" he asks Kim[x] to cover the surge of emotion, turning toward a wall decorated with the figure of a winged virgin in a suggestive pose, flanked by a ram and a lion.

"Welcome to the kingdom of the deep, Magellan[x]," interrupts the husky voice of an old woman still half-concealed by the shadows.

Orante[x], doing his best to act natural, turns around to shake the hand of a bony, shaven-headed individual with a tattoo of a scorpion on his forehead. On the surface of the Vivarium, astrology is considered a mere remnant of Old Earth's confused past. *The Vivarium is the future of Mankind*, after all; no backworlds are needed here.

His eyes finally make out a wheelchair in which an elderly lady with Middle Eastern features sits with taut, straight-backed dignity. A small chameleon sits on her shoulder, oddly watchful. Dressed in a kind of draping, sand-colored gown, she rises unaided, and with unexpected energy. Her plump face creases in an impish smile.

"My name is Aldmira Giga Luna[x]. I'm the double of someone who has been the subject of a great deal of talk lately in Biearth-Paris."

She gestures grandly at the objects piled in the center of the chamber. He notices a small, strange tattoo on her forehead, an image of a blue lobster.

"You recognize these objects, don't you?"

"Yes."

"We have reassembled them for you, largely from our archives, hidden in the no man's land. The Red Ant brought them here." She gestures to a young man with red hair, who holds a bag of salt and vinegar potato chips.

"You were very familiar with the originals of these items a decade ago," she continues. "They were in the bedroom of your old playmate, Angelot. Orante[x], we know you're one of the doubles of a man called Nuno, who used to be Malaner's best friend."

"We were ten years old."

"That is the age for friendship. Maybe the only one."

He gazes at the jumble of objects, shaken. On the other side of the wall, Nuno's heart beats faster as childhood memories take shape in his mind. Kim[x] comes closer to his character, winding the crank of a small red box she holds in the palm of her hand. Nuno lets the melody penetrate his body. He closes his eyes.

Aldmira Giga Luna[x] sits back down in the wheelchair and is silent for a few seconds, then speaks over the theme from *Love Story*:

"What do you think? I'm not sure the music box is identical. We recreated it based on an interview Malaner[x] recently gave, and on archives from the 1970s. But let's get down to business. I want Nuno[x] to become partners with Angelot[x]. Not necessarily out of sentimentality."

"Then why?"

"As a matter of revolutionary strategy."

2
The salvational word

A dog barks in the half-light, a few meters away. Nuno[x] feels only a faint sensation of danger, overridden by the beginnings of euphoria. The early-morning fog covering Biearth-Paris, the blackbird-song, something impenetrable in the eyes of the passers-by—it all seems to indicate that Paridaiza is becoming more and more infused with its real-life model; time stands still sometimes, in bubbles of nothingness.

Mick Flipp[x] is waiting for him in one of the rounded corners of the park in the Place de la Trinité. He is a young man with fine red hair and a cheerful face, dressed in jeans and sneakers. He claps Nuno[x] on the shoulder as if they're old friends:

"Come on, the apartment isn't far. They're waiting for us."

They walk back up the rue d'Athènes. Mick[x] lives on the ground floor of a building whose gray façade is stained with faux traces of pollution. Silently they cross the entry hall, its sandstone walls decorated with green sconces. The apartment door stands half-open.

A female voice straight out of a 1960s pop record sings "*Baby love, how I need you!*" inside. Seated on the bed to the right of Clara[x], Ludwig Flipp[x] looks slightly older than his brother Mick[x]. His build is athletic, his face oblong, and he wears narrow wire-framed glasses. He is manifestly well-suited for the role of group theoretician; when he speaks it is with a slightly affected air, raking his hand through his hair every few minutes.

Because it was Clara[x] who organized this meeting Nuno[x] doesn't feel wary, only a bit nervous. Gripping a multicolored Rubik's similicube in his left hand to calm himself, he looks around the room: a bamboo bed, two lamps emitting a rosy light, three white pine chairs, a wrought-iron table holding a Thermos and some chrome-plated cups.

Clara[x] takes his right hand tenderly. "We're putting a lot of faith in Magellan's descendant."

⌘

Three hours later, alone on the street again, Nuno[x] bursts out laughing. The people calling themselves the "Hazardous Intraterrestrials!" have assigned him a project far crazier than their petty attacks, which are effectively meant to pass them off as simple pranksters, as Clara[x] revealed, dropping a light kiss on his forehead. But now, HI! wants to kidnap Ludmila Gagarina[x].

Why?

On Old Earth, the Nobel Prize, drawing on the work of the neo-Darwinists, conducted a disturbing experiment a few years ago. Nuno[x] doesn't fully understand

86

exactly what happened; it was apparently something to do with the coding units of human DNA. Then all that was needed was to compose a message inside a stubborn virus, and then inject this virus into the body of an individual who would then infect the people around them by sneezing or exchanging saliva or other bodily fluids.

And then?

During an experiment conducted in August 2010 at the Natural History Museum of Paris, Gagarina coded the first sentence of the Gospel according to Saint John into the blood of a male rhesus monkey living with a female. A few months later, a baby monkey was born in the zoo at the Jardin des Plantes, a dormant part of whose DNA carried the famous phrase, "In the beginning was the Word."

So?

The Hazardous Intraterrestrials are convinced that Gagarina's experiment could prove much more effective in Paridaiza. Transposing the operation in the form of an instruction built into the lines of code controlling the game could make it possible to interfere with its fascistic sequencing. Certain words, repeated over and over again, act as *agents provocateurs*; they are the truest form of human energy. In the beginning is indeed the Word. But which one?

The introduction of an unexpected microcode into a world like Paridaiza could foster the emergence of something different, something free, or mad, or more varied. Even better, thanks to the gateway of the Sensorium, this verbal grain of sand could influence players in real life. The next stage, in HI!'s ambitious and fanciful plan, will therefore consist of "proposing" that Gagarina help them to transpose her technique into the world of Biearth via a consenting character, a double who has access to the Vivarium: Orante Magellan[x].

As for the grain of sand introduced into Paridaiza's machinery, it would be a "salvational" word chosen at random from the dictionary. Just a single word, Clara[x] said, enthusiastically:

"A whole phrase, a maxim, for example, even "Love one another", would just be another fascistic tangle."

On the other side of the screen, barely recovered from his encounter with Aldmira Giga Luna[x], Nuno can't quite understand what's happening to him anymore. He feels amused, proud, and disoriented all at once. Why do so many people want to assign him a revolutionary role? A few months ago he would never have thought that giving a simple computer-game avatar the name of a famous navigator would get him into so many strange situations. Is that the magic word? Magellan?

"After the operation," Ludwig[x] added, all Magellan[x] will have to is spread his virus in the game, hoping to be the butterfly that might cause—through the Sensorium—a tornado of human liberation. Anarchy will triumph. We must have a blank slate, before we can rebuild."

"Mmm. If we can prevent Love Day, even that would be pretty good," says Clara[x], more conservatively.

"But why are you so negative about the Amorium?" asked Nuno[x].

"Because neuronal stimulation acts like a drug. In the beginning, it seems to have a positive effect. But over time, the opposite becomes true. Paradise becomes a kind of hell."

Clara[x] came closer to Nuno[x]. "And what, my dear," she murmured, "is the opposite of love?"

V
Fusion

1
Love Story

Every day on the rue de la Gaîté, the Mirror Museum, popularized by Gagarina[x], receives more visitors than the neighboring sex shops. They marvel at the purity of the precious looking-glasses. Sometimes the couples will try, not without nervous laughter, to see if their reflection will light up, confirming their status as soulmates, while the children make goofy faces in front of the funhouse mirrors. A few enthusiasts make their first forays into specular science by purchasing, in the museum's small bookshop, a facsimile copy of a Leonardo da Vinci manuscript written in mirror-script, or backwards. Magellan[x] has often leafed through the book, stopping more and more frequently on a phrase that fills him with a sense of foreboding:

> *If you take eight flat mirrors, each two fathoms wide and three fathoms high, and arrange these in a circle to as to create an octagon, the perimeter of which shall be sixteen fathoms and the diameter five fathoms,*

*a man placed in the center shall be able to
see himself from all sides, an infinite number
of times.*

This is in fact quite similar to the description of a mirodrome. Mirodromes, used mainly during the past few decades for erotic purposes, are becoming increasingly rare in Europe's red-light districts, with the preference now being for pornographic holograms. What troubles Nuno is that there is still a mirodrome on the rue de la Gaîté, no more than twenty meters from the museum, in Victoria's Sex Shop. At first glance, there doesn't seem to be anything infinite about the place . . .

Girls provide strip-teases there in five- or ten-minute sessions, dancing under a red light, visibly weary, smiling mechanically, diluting their awareness in a bath of techno drumbeats. They enter the octagon through a door hung with a simple mirror.

Seven two-way mirrors each open into a private booth equipped with a coin-slot mechanism. The woman at the center of the octagon can only see the customers in the booths as vague silhouettes that blur together with her own endlessly-multiplied reflection. Reclining on a rotating platform, removing item after item of clothing, it's her job to arouse desire in the phantoms occupying these booths for as long as they keep feeding coins into the slots.

The mirror is a world, thinks Nuno, on the other side of the screen. People sometimes take it for just a small narcissistic object, but it has also been used as a weapon, as the museum's brochure explains. Before

94

the invention of gunpowder, people tried to imitate Archimedes by using large "burning glasses" to set fire to their opponents. Panoptic batteries were constructed to defend besieged cities. The sun's rays hit these mirrors obliquely and were reflected back toward the enemy's position, setting tents and ammunition aflame *ab igne mathematico*, struck down by "mathematical fire".

And in ancient Greece, the mirror was complicit with desire, an instrument of Eros—on the subject of which god the museum's bookshop also carries an illustrated edition of Perrault's 1661 tale *The Mirror, or The Metamorphosis of Orante*, a story Nuno has come to know by heart.

Orante is a first name that comes from the ancient Greek and means "the one who shows" as well as "the seer". The Orante in Perrault's tale possesses a certain talent for frank and innocent descriptions of what he sees, particularly portraits of courtiers, yet he lacks memory and judgment, forgetting about a thing the moment it leaves his field of vision, and unable to keep from saying absolutely everything that comes into his mind. He cannot—or will not—adjust his point of view, which earns him more than one enemy.

This, of course, results in drama. Caliste, the young woman he loves, and of whom he reflects such a beautiful image that she can't keep away from him, is gradually disfigured by smallpox. Orante reveals to her, without tact but also without malice, the unsightly changes to her face, which her friends try to play down:

"Am I so ugly as all that?"

"You are frightful."

This isn't the most diplomatic of answers, and it causes the despairing Caliste to stab Orante with an awl. He falls to the ground, his body stiff and cold as glass. It's then that the god Eros, who was observed the scene, transforms Orante into a mirror. The moral of the story: there is nothing that can't be looked at in several ways.

Tonight, in his studio, Nuno thinks about this story. He has always thought of himself as seeking a fixed axis; a solid, active way of looking at the world, an open-minded view, fertile but intangible. But are we ever really immune to appearances?

When Orante saw Caliste's altered face, did he stop loving her?

Orante[x] has, two or three times, at the end of his shift at the museum, gone into Victoria's and shut himself into one of the mirodrome's booths. It's not the most exciting form of exhibition he knows of, but the panoptic device fascinates him. It almost seems to him like a metaphor for the modern quest for identity, a sort of Allegory of the Cave for these times—well, as much as a stripper can be an allegory for anything.

Sometimes he tries to make out the facial expressions of the men barely hidden behind the other mirrors, but they're only faint specters whose presence he can only sense through the gaze of the nude female avatar and the vague gestures she makes toward them as she rotates inside the circular chamber.

Melody[x], announces a ridiculous voice over a microphone, is the stage name of the young woman swaying her hips beneath Orante[x]'s eyes this evening. The character looks twenty-five years old at most. Her slightly rounded face with its luminous complexion is topped by a mass of fair hair. Her eyes sparkle. Magellan[x] is surprised to find a being so pure in appearance imprisoned in the mirodrome. Little by little he feels a sensation of peace overtaking him, though he can't tell if it's caused by Melody[x]'s smile, the rosy tints of her skin under the red neon lights, or the graceful curves of her body. Is she smiling directly at him?

Behind the double he is controlling, Nuno feels a strangely familiar thrill run down his spine. He isn't hearing the sex-shop music anymore. There is an angel here, a ghost he wants to liberate, even if it means breaking the screens . . .

Everything speeds up. He fidgets in his booth when Melody[x] leaves the mirodrome's stage. Now it is Deborah[x]'s turn to display her virtual anatomy. The feeling of indifference returns; he watches the show without seeing it for a minute or two, and eventually leaves the booth, head down.

Melody[x] is dressed now, in a red coat and an orange scarf. She reaches the sex shop door at the same time as him. Seeing her freed from her prison revives his curiosity. He follows her.

A few meters away, she takes the stairs down into the Edgar-Quinet similimetro station. He trails after her to the platform, mesmerized. But how do you approach a strange woman whom you've just seen completely naked? The train appears, slows down, stops. He leaps in front of the young woman and grabs the metal door-handle, turning to her with an impish smile.

"Let me get that for you!"

The girl smiles back. They sit down next to each other and strike up a conversation, harmless but tinged with flirtation. A few seconds before the Denfert-Rochereau stop, she agrees to go for a drink. They walk back up to street level, talking about the Mirror Museum, which she says she has never visited.

Magellan^x's consciousness is flooded by a wave of confused, pleasant, almost hallucinatory impressions. Everything seems to be quivering around him. It's as if the ground is dissolving beneath his feet, as if a sticky resin, a shallow torrent of lava is flowing imperceptibly toward the Apollo bar, located in a former railway shunting yard a few meters from the statue of the *Lion de Belfort*. Why this noticeable blurring? Is it emotion? A premonition?

Or the first manifestation of Paridaiza's side effects?

They sit outside on the patio. The money Melody^x earns in the mirodrome, it turns out, allows the mysterious Internet user controlling her to pay for voice lessons on Old Earth. She admits that she is taking classes in a conservatory just outside Paris, hoping to become a professional soprano and to appear, at least once in her life, on the operatic stage. Orante^x avoids mentioning the Vivarium, where you hear the theme from *Love Story,* in the slow electronic version that has become the anthem of the Pleasurium, far more often than Mozart's *Cosi fan tutte.*

He finds himself drowning in her eyes. He asks what she thinks about the Soulmate fad and Love Day. Her face darkens.

"But they'd have to have a soul for that."

"You aren't looking for Prince Charming?"

"I love the male human body. Sex makes me zen, but I don't like the word *zen* . . ."

A silence.

She runs the fingers of her right hand lightly over her own left palm.

He watches her, more and more fascinated. She closes her eyes. Her fingers are long and slim. Orante[x] wonders if her similiskin tastes like milk and vanilla. He slides his hand over hers. She doesn't pull it away. He asks her real first name.

"My name really is Mélodie[x], but with an e. Like the French for *song*."

Behind the Sensorium interface, Clara smiles at the lie by omission, at the same time feeling slightly jealous of her own new avatar.

Nuno doesn't deserve to learn right away that she is the one who created Mélodie[x] nine days ago. And she's even less likely to mention the recent encounter between Mélodie[x] and a certain Angelot[x].

Half an hour later, Magellan[x] and Mélodie[x] are on the verge of kissing at the foot of the proud *Lion de Belfort*, but she suddenly backs away and hurries off without a word, leaving Orante[x] alone and pale as a statue.

Nothing now but to go home in a state of melancholy confusion. The streets seem more deserted than usual; the things happening around him mere grains of sand between his fingers. The moon isn't quite full. He is annoyed with himself, interpreting Mélodie[x]'s flight as a failure, a rookie mistake. *I probably moved too fast*, he thinks. *Scared her off.*

Behind his double, Nuno also feels slightly guilty for having momentarily forgotten Clara. If he only knew that she had just been testing him, and that he had failed the test.

Back at home, the feelings of confusion and loneliness continue. Then, suddenly, his phone pings with a text message from HI!, signed by Ludwig[x]: *Gagarina[x] is giving a talk at the château in Biearth-Nantes. Kidnapping possible.*

Nuno takes a deep breath. Nothing like preparing for a revolution to make you forget about your woman troubles.

In theory, at least.

2
The art of kidnapping

The building in which Vivarium's parliament meets is a dome constructed of similititanium and silica. Above the lower chamber where the sixty Ultras elected for a one-year term meet, two men and one woman with geometrically symmetrical features rendered excessively smooth by Transparency are seated in the seated at the center of an immense room with a domed ceiling. They stand up when Angelot Malaner[x] enters.

He seems a bit nervous, especially in contrast to his interlocutors, who maintain the elite's customary appearance of calm. Parliamentarians sometimes go so far as to claim, not unhypocritically, that they have reasserted the ancient Romans' four cardinal values: *industria, gravitas, severitas,* and *constantia.* Work, gravity, severity, and constancy. Words that have unfortunately become parodies of themselves, thinks Malaner[x]. He considers most of his contemporaries, including the Ultras, to represent four other qualities instead: inconstancy, evanescence, fear, and dishonesty.

He sits up straighter in his chair and assumes a more relaxed position; he mustn't risk blemishing his reputation as a young man of easy grace. Some Internet users say he's too ambitious, but everyone agrees that he is extremely good at the difficult practice of being brainy and charming at the same time.

To tell the truth, however, a crack has recently opened up in his self-esteem. For the first time in his life, he feels almost like a fraud; he cannot shake the idea that the Amorium isn't in perfect working order yet, and that its effects are uncertain. He and his research team can only claim with certainty that they have pinpointed the neuronal zone where love occurs; at the very most, they have managed to inhibit certain egotistical behaviors and to provoke fleeting bursts of compassion in their test subjects. As for side effects . . . In all honesty, they should push the December 21st date back by a year and conduct more experiments. But Godpreview needs more and more money, and the parliamentarians, as well as Malaner's associates on Old Earth, have no intention of upsetting their investors.

Despite the quartz-encrusted anthracite suit that dials up his natural elegance even further, today he feels a slight sense of shame. So, he will have to yield to that liberal practice that consists of launching unfinished products for which their consumers will thus become the guinea pigs. He has always enjoyed earning money through his own merit in the past, and this inability to delay Love Day feels like a derailment, so much so that he is sometimes seized with the desire to smash his own toy—an idea he never envisions without a rather pleasurable shiver of terror.

Right now he would like nothing more than to go home and sit at his piano and think. He looks around, overwhelmed with a sudden feeling of disgust. The gleaming facial skin of the parliamentary representatives gives their expressions a disturbingly reflective quality. With a slow, magisterial movement, the woman dabs a bead of sweat off her face with a tissue.

"There's someone we'd like to introduce to you, Malaner[x]. Madam Aldmira Giga Luna[x] has apparently been wanting to meet you for quite some time."

He turns and looks with surprise at an old woman with Persian features who is wheeled slowly into the room by an assistant. A small chameleon with bulging eyes slips from Giga Luna[x]'s shoulder and, with a few flicks of its tail, freezes in the center of the conference table, warily observing the characters surrounding it.

When the rebel leader emerged from the depths of the Vivarium, claiming to be the chief of a group of fifty Antisocials responsible for the Reminibus attacks and now ready to act against the Pleasurium's software, Parliament, far from panicking, realized that this was a perfect opportunity—before plunging Aldmira Giga Luna[x] into The Great Night—to distract Malaner[x] from his misgivings. The Ultras haven't been taking the threats and proposals for negotiation put out by the rebels very seriously, but they have now decided to apply an old diplomatic ruse: when two secondary powers begin to become bothersome, make it so that they cancel each other out.

"We have no reason to believe you're anything but a pathological liar," says Angelot[x], aiming a dark look at the old woman. "And what exactly are you trying to accomplish?"

"You're asking two questions at once, Malaner[x]. That's never a smart move; it means I only have to answer the question I find less annoying. You're going to have to let go of your old instincts. The world has changed; *friend* and *enemy* are outdated terms. You'd do well to understand that, aspiring as you do to usher the human race into some kind of superior reality. The least you can do at the moment is admit to yourself that the Antisocials are capable of taking action—in spite of The Great Night, which has taken a mere tenth of our operatives."

Unexpectedly, Angelot[x] smiles faintly. He feels suddenly calmer; his quick mind has just glimpsed a way out. But he darts a discreet glance at the parliamentarians and replies, feigning an alarmist tone:

"In concrete terms, what are you planning to do?"

"After several months of work we are at the point of being able to connect, without being noticed, to the computers that control the operation of the Pleasurium."

Malaner[x] pauses for a beat. Then he turns theatrically toward the parliamentarians:

"Why haven't you gotten rid of this person yet?"

"We don't take orders from you, Angelot[x]," one of the two men replies. "With all due respect, it's still Parliament that makes those decisions. Something you tend to forget."

Giga Luna[x] continues, imperturbable:

"I don't want to alarm you, but the pretty chameleon you see on the table before you is a transmitter. This meeting is being recorded. And if anything happens to me, in less than one hour our technicians will plunge the Absolux tower into darkness."

Angelot[x] loses his sangfroid. "You've gone to all this trouble to come here and mock me before you act? You're bluffing."

They both fall silent beneath the distant gazes of the three parliamentarians, each trying to read the mind of the other. On the conference table, the chameleon perches unmoving; only its little head and its large eyes move, scanning the room's décor. The truth, which the old rebel is keeping to herself, is that the pirates trying to develop a virus that will corrupt Absolux's programs haven't yet managed to decrypt the codes safeguarding the Pleasurium.

There is actually a less technical reason for Giga Luna[x]'s suicidal appearance here. She wants to make Malaner[x] understand that the Ultras, including his Godpreview colleagues, have become suspicious of his ambition, and thus contributed to the switching of camps by Paridaiza's best programmer. But why?

The chameleon jumps off the table to the floor and climbs up the wheelchair's tire to return to the old woman's shoulder.

"What are your group's demands?" asks Angelot[x], feigning indifference again now.

"It's quite simple, Malaner[x]," answers Giga Luna[x] before turning and starting for the door. "We just want you to meet with the double of a childhood friend, someone who knows you extremely well. The rest, you'll find out when the time is right."

"If we give you the time," puts in one of the parliamentarians, with a smirk.

⌘

Ludwig[x] rummages in his rucksack and extracts a set of Breaker Cobra binoculars on which Nuno[x] can make out the logo of two red eagles. The muscular and intellectual HI! operative is dressed in a khaki shirt and trousers that give him the look of a soldier on leave. The shirt has an embroidered inscription in indecipherable golden characters. Nuno[x] asks him about it.

"*The world is your improvisation*," Ludwig[x] explains. "Translated from the ancient Avestan. Like Paradise for Paridaiza, you see."

The two men cross a metal platform on the second floor of the Eiffel Tower. Nuno[x], impatient, asks Ludwig[x] how HI! is planning on getting close enough to Gagarina[x] to kidnap her; assuming she agrees to become part of their virus project, that is.

"It's simple. Four students working as receptionists for the Elegancia[x] agency will have to be hired to work the symposium at the Biearth-Nantes château. They'll wear purple suits and a badge like this"—he takes a yellow plastic rectangle out of his shirt pocket. "We've spoken to one of them who, for a fee, will allow herself to be replaced at the last minute by Mélodie[x]."

"Mélodie[x]?"

"Yeah, Clara's second double. Didn't you know?"

106

Nuno[x] tries to hide his surprise and turns quickly to survey the horizon. On the other side of the screen, Nuno's heart starts pounding.

Ludwig[x] keeps talking, an odd smile on his face. "In exactly ten days, at around noon, Mélodie[x] will approach Gagarina[x] at the end of her presentation and direct her to an isolated room on the ground floor, supposedly for an interview that has been previously arranged with a special envoy from *Time-Paridaiza*, who will actually be Mick[x]."

"You think a Nobel Prize winner will be so easy to fool?" asks Nuno[x], his mind elsewhere.

"Mélodie[x] will bombard her with compliments on her little Soulmate theory, to gain her trust. Then, while Mick[x] is distracting her with a question, Mélodie[x] will quickly inject her in the shoulder from behind with a microsyringe of concentrated olanzapine."

"A microsyringe of what?"

The other man smiles again. "Olanzapine. They use it on Old Earth to treat schizophrenia. It inhibits nervous system activity. But our olanzapine is just the code name for a computer microvirus you can buy pretty easily on the hacking black market."

Nuno is having trouble concentrating on his avatar. He can't stop thinking about the naked body of Mélodie[x] swaying lasciviously in the mirodrome at Victoria's. Has Clara, on the other side of the mirror, developed a taste for strip-teasing?

Ludwig[x] continues, his expression serious now. "In a few seconds, Gagarina[x]'s pulse should slow down. She'll become sleepy. Mick[x] and Mélodie[x] will take her out the door and along a corridor to a staircase that goes down to the château's cellar. There's a passage from there leading into the sewers."

"The dirty bitch!"

"What?"

". . . uh, I mean, how dirty, the sewers . . ."

Mélodie[x]'s sudden withdrawal last night, at the foot of the leonine statue in the similiplace Denfert-Rocheau, makes more sense to Nuno now. Men are nothing but helpless infants when it comes to women's schemes . . .

Ludwig[x] keeps talking enthusiastically. "Fifty meters along, they'll reach an underground cistern that supplies the city center. You and I will be waiting there to help them get Gagarina[x] out. Orante[x], on Autopilot, will be parked behind the southern wing of the château in a van with the logo of an air-conditioning company painted on it. The whole operation won't cost much at all; two thousand paridollars, tops."

Nuno[x] doesn't find the kidnap plan feasible at all. He wonders if the real Ludwig is beginning to mix up reality and virtuality, as gradually happens to the game's best players. This business about an injection slowing down the pulse of a computer avatar seems ridiculous to him.

It's really nothing more than the transposition of Gagarina's experiments on DNA to the virtual world, in the end, right?

⌘

The Sunflower is a bar on the Biearth-rue de la Gaîté reproduced to perfection, with its antique sofas, ovoid lamps, and yellowish walls hung with bright orange wild dagga plants. Mélodie[x] and Orante[x] are seated at the counter. She looks at him, shyly.

"You can't fall in love with me. I'm living with a man."

Who's living with a man? Clara?

"Of course not, Mélodie[x] . . ."

The conversation could stop there; one more set of parentheses opened and never closed. He could try to forget Mélodie[x] and his thoughts would return selflessly to his mission for HI!. To changing the world. Compared to an important aim like that, what did the ups and downs and avatars matter of a romance that would end up, like so many others, as intensely negative as a black hole?

And moreover, despite his misgivings, he is feeling more and more proud to be a chief player in such a revolutionary plan, even with its risks. For the last few days, in an attempt to broaden his mind, he has been opening his dictionary at random, closing his eyes and pointing to a word.

Could one simple word really become a virus, powerful enough to infect Paridaiza and, indirectly, Earth too? There is a problem; most of the words he has found himself pointing at don't seem to possess the slightest magical power or ideological significance: chair, karaoke, lotion. The idea of transforming a signifier into a technological imperative also seems quite unpredictable. And he has no desire to have the innermost part of his being tattooed with a code that lacks panache.

Behind the mask of Orante[x], In Nuno's mind, an alternative idea begins to announce its presence. But it would mean betraying his new friends.

The tête-à-tête with Mélodie[x], as disagreeable as it has become, will have to continue. She tells him that the man she fell in love with a few weeks ago, and whom she calls "my sweetheart" with no apparent regard for Orante[x]'s feelings, manages—among other things—a small simili-artisanal workshop in a suburb of Biearth-Paris.

"And he doesn't mind your working at Victoria's, your sweetheart?" Orante[x] asks, half ironic, half deflated.

Mélodie[x]'s face lights up.

"He's asked me to stop."

"He's going to pay for your voice studies?"

"No, I want to work. He's going to train me to produce his music boxes. They're beautiful, you'll see; luxurious, exquisitely crafted."

"Do these pseudo-boxes have a brand name?"

"Absolux. Like the Absolux tower, which my sweetheart Angelot[x] runs when he's in the Vivarium."

Let it never be said that a Magellan cannot hide his weaknesses. Naturally, casually, he signals to the waitress and orders.

"A Kalashni . . . sorry, I mean, a vodka, please."

When he gave Angelot's grandfather's little red music box to Clara a few months ago, he would never have imagined that the two would meet one day, much less that they'd be sleeping together, albeit via their doubles in Paridaiza.

110

Is this just one of Clara's ruses to make Nuno jealous, or are the two people who have, up to now, been dearest to him in the world on the verge of leaving him behind?

⌘

Passing through the Painting Room at the Mirror Museum shortly before its 2:00 pm opening time, Orante Magellan[x] contemplates a reproduction of Hieronymus Bosch's *Garden of Earthly Delights*. A finely painted crystal surface covers the hindquarters of a monstrous figure crawling beneath Satan's throne and illustrating the medieval proverb, "When you look in the mirror, you are looking up the Devil's arse."

A woman with dangling arms is reflected there, narcissistic, a toad between her breasts, lulled to sleep by her disturbed thoughts.

Maybe Nuno should let go of his jealousy. In a world where schizoneurosis and role-playing games are gradually becoming the norm, there's something archaic about clinging to the tradition of monogamous romantic relationships, perhaps. After all, he tries to reassure himself, if he loves Clara and respects Angelot, why not be happy that they are together, which, when you consider that excellence attracts excellence, shouldn't even come as that much of a surprise.

On the other hand, it irritates him that he didn't think of introducing them himself. He has no desire to be a plaything of destiny.

The previous evening, after his meeting with Mélodie[x], finding and writing down Gagarina[x]'s contact information took no more than a few seconds; the propagandist of Soulmates has her own place in Paridaiza. Logically speaking, he thinks, despite having had it forced on her, the scientist should actually be delighted to be part of HI!'s plan, which may give her the opportunity to conduct a large-scale repetition of her experiments in genetic coding while at the same time enabling her to protest that she had been compelled by microterrorists to do it, if things went wrong. But the choice of a virus at random might not satisfy the Nobel laureate's strict code of conduct—at least, he hopes it won't. And so he doesn't think it would be unreasonable to contact her secretly, unbeknownst to his colleagues, and collaborate with her in choosing the actual verbal instruction she will etch into the coding lines of Magellan[x]'s DNA. The word *freedom*, for example.

Freedom is a lovelier word than *karaoke*, no question. But will such an idealistic command have the desired effect? And, more than that, will Orante[x] be capable of betraying the people who have put their trust in him?

Standing in front of Bosch's painting, he feels close to renouncing his vague plans for political disloyalty, the prospect of which makes him anxious. He doesn't think his own idea is any more unrealistic than HI!'s. Who can claim to understand the true power of a word? A grouping of letters like *freedom* or *equality* once had the power to electrify crowds on Old Earth, if spoken by a passionate and charismatic orator. But do Paridaiza's players, deep down inside themselves, really even want to be free?

He wonders if he should simply allow himself to be carried along by whatever happens, let himself be used as a new, unpredictable type of humanoid bomb. And forget Mélodie[x]—or rather, accept that Clara loves Nuno[x] when she's Clara, and Angelot[x] when she's Mélodie[x]. And . . . Nuno when she's Clara?

The museum director is dressed today in his nattiest three-piece suit. He calls the staff together before the museum opens. He is a short, dry man whose parchment-like, faintly gleaming skin looks embalmed. He speaks solemnly:

"Today is an important day for the museum. I received a call this morning from an American television network, and I have given permission for an interview with Ludmila Gagarina[x] to take place late this afternoon in the Panoptic Room. I'm counting on you; the world will be watching!"

It appears that the Nobel laureate's double will be asked one more time about her vision for Love Day, the link between collective love and love between two beings, and mirrors that light up in the presence of Soulmates. Orante[x] spends the rest of the afternoon feeling rattled at this sign that fate seems to be sending, a decidedly facetious one, by serving the scientist up to him on a platter this way. He only has a few moments left to decide whether or not to speak to her in private.

Five o'clock that evening sees a crowd of one hundred pacing from room to room, impatiently awaiting its idol. The meeting between Gagarina[x] and the American television crew is scheduled to take place in less than an hour.

Thirty minutes later the crew appears, preceded by the museum director. Behind the camera, the boom microphone, and the array of electronic equipment, Orante[x] is astonished to recognize Ludwig[x], Mick[x], and Clara[x]. The latter winks at him. He responds with a shaky smile. So they have managed to trap her with their Nantes château, and he is quite obviously no longer in control of his own simililife. Everyone seems prepared to betray him. Or maybe *betray* is too strong a word.

Gagarina[x] arrives right on time, already followed by a mob of admirers. She is dressed, mockingly perhaps, in a violet silk Indian sari that makes her look like a guru. The interview starts off smoothly, but then a more and more dense crowd begins to press in around the Nobel laureate's avatar, throwing the Panoptic Room into confusion. Orante[x] is held back from action by the presence of his fatherly boss next to him, observing the scene with satisfaction, arms crossed, nodding along with Gagarina[x]'s responses.

After several minutes, Ludwig[x], holding the boom mike, says audibly to Clara[x], "We've got a problem with the sound."

Wearing his most impish smile, Mick[x] leans toward Gagarina[x]. "May we kidnap you for just a moment and take you out to our broadcasting van? Just to finish the interview under proper conditions."

⌘

Eight days earlier, in the Vivarium, on the top floor of the Absolux tower, Malaner^x abandoned himself once more to the soothing touch of Kim^x. Since his troubling encounter with Aldmira Giga Luna^x in the Parliament building, Angelot^x had been torn between two contradictory hopes.

"You seem tense," the young Asian woman remarked. "Divided."

In any other circumstances he would never have confided in her, but the warmth of Kim^x's hands had weakened his defenses. "That Luna^x . . ." he mumbled, as if speaking to himself.

"Are you hoping to see her again?"

"I think so. But not anywhere near Parliament . . ."

"That can be arranged, if you'll trust me. I assume you've heard of Gagarina^x, the famous Nobel laureate's avatar?"

It was approaching sunset on that summer day in 2012. Malaner^x would cross paths once more with Aldmira Giga Luna^x, the second avatar controlled by the enigmatic Ludmila Gagarina, that very evening. And as usual, he would make a rapid-fire decision.

The sun sank lower in the Vivarium's sky, absorbed by the horizon of the no man's land surrounding the futuristic city, and descended beneath the waters of the Biearth-Pacific Ocean, seemingly indifferent to the fate of the world.

BOOK TWO

THE STRAIT

I

In the beginning was the Word

1
Blue lobsters

The sun's rays stream through the glass walls of a workshop situated in the suburban heights near the Biearth-Bois de Boulogne. Disemboweled music boxes share space with a clutter of artisanal tools amid the rustic décor. It's Sunday. Mélodie[x], seated at a massive table, is carefully brushing varnish on an inlaid wooden lid she will then screw onto a box in the "Mozart" line. She breathes in the scent of resin and caresses the smooth grain of the similiwood with her palm.

Behind her holographic screen, Clara doesn't know if these sensations are identical to the real thing, since she's never really taken the time to stroke a wooden object on Old Earth, other than the worn keys of old harpsichords with her fingertips. Manual labor, even virtual, is conducive to meditation, allowing her thoughts to wander as it does. But she can't keep herself from smiling; she knows that over the past few days, Nuno[x] has become more possessive toward Clara[x], perhaps partly due to his jealousy of Malaner[x]. The old love-triangle strategy is working perfectly.

She wonders what it is that she really wants, deep down. Something simple and crazy at the same time. To become, by means of Paridaiza, the most important woman in Nuno's life, the heart of his passion, his safe harbor, the refuge to which he will always return, his equator, his North Pole, his Strait of Magellan, his Greenwich Meridian, his marker sign, his green, yellow, and red lights, his information desk, his travel agency, the purveyor of all his dreams and a few nightmares too, his night train, his bedside lamp, his bedside book, his book never finished. And, more concretely, yes, she wants to have a child with him before it's too late. Her body is calling out to her, and it has never called out so loudly as it does when she's with Nuno. But he isn't ready yet. Far from it . . .

With a final inspection, from various angles, Mélodie[x] makes sure the music box is finished. Angelot[x] didn't think she would be such a quick learner, but she has proven to be not only skilled, but meticulous—and passionate to the point of working on days everyone else takes off, as if these music boxes are of extreme importance. Now she reattaches the similispring and the cylinder starts turning, its tiny picots causing the iron strips to oscillate and emit the crystalline sound of a Mozart lullaby.

The first music boxes, created in the early eighteenth century, were minuscule mechanisms contained in snuffboxes. They were mass-produced, somewhat like the Walkman many years later, and enjoyed great popularity until the gramophone replaced them. Today they are regarded as antiquated luxury items. The film and television industries have frequently used them in the sort of horror stories where children are possessed by demons, for which the viewing public seems to have lost its taste in recent years. Now, a few nostalgia-peddlers in Paridaiza are beginning to offer these precious machines again, boasting that they have been "handmade"—an irony of the game—without a single electronic component.

What Clara appreciates about the sound of Absolux boxes is that they seem to combine extreme lightness with a depth that she finds profoundly moving, though she can come up with no clear explanation for its very real charm. It gives a strange impression of presence, as if the box is somehow peacefully alive. Malaner is certainly a man of many talents.

Is Clara truly cheating on Nuno with him when Malaner[x] makes love with Mélodie[x] via the Pleasurium? Whenever the question pops into her head, invariably making her slightly uncomfortable, she tries to keep from thinking about it too much by singing Bizet's *Carmen* under her breath. Is love really a wild bird that no one can tame?

⌘

Is this still a personal, private journal? Sometimes I'm Nuno, sometimes Magellan[x], sometimes Nuno[x], sometimes someone else entirely, and it's like I think that, by multiplying myself so much, I'll be able somehow to get rid of my premature boredom with reality.

But I don't always understand what's happening to me, except that my lives go on, interlaced, while my soul seems to exist in a third universe, which seems neither blandly real *nor* coldly virtual.

But whenever Nuno[x] is with Clara[x], my anxiety returns. I've been lying to myself up to now; I don't feel love from her the way I used to. I need to see Clara again, outside the game . . .

⌘

With two months to go until Love Day, in Paridaiza, the widely-publicized disappearance of Ludmila Gagarina[x] almost completely overshadows an event which, at any other time, would have been the talk of the town: the appearance in the Biearth-Paris Seine of several hundred blue lobsters. But, given the circumstances, the only hint of controversy stirred by this strange proliferation occurs when several prominent restaurants, attracted by the rarity and unique taste of the cobalt crustacean, protest City Hall's monopoly on the rights to its capture.

On Old Earth, only one lobster in a million possesses a blue carapace, the result of a genetic mutation. It is thought that the color provides better camouflage in the water and a less appetizing appearance for predators, an advantage that intrigues evolutionists since it hasn't yet caused an increase in blue shells to the detriment of other colors, which seems to fly in the face of Darwinist theory. Some creationists have even claimed that this arthropodan anomaly proves the existence of

God. Yet, shouldn't the conflict between evolutionists and creationists have been consigned to the dustbin of history on Paridaiza by now?

The large number of blue lobsters in the artificially foul-smelling waters of the Seine is something less than a miracle. Rather, the maintenance team at the small vivarium located in a zoo building in the Jardin des Plantes—this vivarium, with a lower-case 'v', consists of a series of glass cases filled with snakes and spiders as well as the aforementioned arthropods—has just publicly admitted its responsibility for the release of several dozen blue lobsters into the river. To the astonishment of the zoo's management, the animals had quickly begun reproducing at extremely high speed in their glass prison, for no apparent reason.

⌘

Sometimes I feel like I'm not drifting so much anymore. Actually, I feel a growing sense of pride. I feel a pure yearning for adventure, for unveiling. And I feel less misanthropic, less isolated from everyone else.

But these feelings only come when I'm alone. Yesterday Clara agreed to go for a drink with me. We met in a café on the Ile Saint-Louis. We talked, we smiled. But after I left her I felt empty, almost anxious. And tired out, too, by the effort it took me to really be there, with her. I felt like there was a glass screen separating us, like we were just pretending to be a couple again.

⌘

Equally inexplicably, the vegetation in the Jardin des Plantes has recently been growing abnormally fast. Despite it being early autumn, the flora is getting denser by the day, palm trees sprouting up even on the footpaths and plants growing rampant over the sidewalks. While children exuberantly turn cartwheels on the plush carpet of greenery and climb the vines above the Quai Saint-Bernard, their parents eye the strange botanical deluge warily, even suspiciously.

Only esotericism and romanticism seem able, these days, to make people forget the technique of taking plant-cuttings, and human imagination has never lacked the ability to make up fantastical explanations for things. For example, some websites are speculating that the accelerated growth is a divine omen, a pronouncement of the coming of Love prophesied by the Mayans for December 21, 2012.

But the soberest experts are proposing another theory: a mysterious virus is being propagated in Paridaiza. The computer codes controlling the game's environment may have been altered by pirates, something that Godpreview Incorporated continues to deny, for now.

⌘

The eminent kidnapping victim, woken and untied by Ludwig[x] a few seconds ago, sits up and stretches, smiling. Clara[x], Nuno[x], and Mick[x] are seated in front of her in the studio on the rue d'Athènes, more awkward than threatening. Orante[x], slightly off to one side and deep in the limbo of Autopilot mode, has a dictionary in his lap.

The scientist has just confessed to the "not at all unpleasant" young people who made off with her avatar a week ago that she is responsible for the proliferation of the blue lobsters.

She is behind the increased growth of the Jardin des Plantes flora as well—along with her two accomplices. One of them is Kim[x], a researcher at the Museum of Natural History who has temporarily been acting as a masseuse in order to infiltrate the island of the Ultras. And Gagarina[x]'s second accomplice, a very recent recruit, is none other than the celebrated Malaner[x]. Without his technological knowledge, she would never have managed, 24 hours before her kidnapping by HI!, to transpose her DNA experiments into the world of Paridaiza in the form of a digital and alphabetical virus.

Convincing Angelot Malaner[x] to help them was no easy job. It even required the sacrifice of her best double, Aldmira Giga Luna[x], whom she used as bait and is now rotting in The Great Night. Yet Parliament has never managed to discern Gagarina[x] behind the character of the spiritual leader of the Antisocials—again, thanks to the talents of Malaner[x].

"He's arrogant but he has a good heart," the scientist now insists to her stunned captors. "He was a bit disappointed by the reality of power. But he's still a bit of a loose cannon. I'm counting on his old friendship with Nuno to win him over completely."

"You should probably count on Mélodie[x] for that instead," observes Nuno[x], sourly.

There is an awkward silence. Clara[x] laughs, a bit nervously. There are tears in her eyes. She stands up, goes over to Nuno[x], acts as if she's about to slap him—but caresses his cheek gently instead.

⌘

It's like I was this *close to understanding how things work, to tearing away the veil of illusion. But the rug keeps getting pulled out from under me. I look out the library window at a gleaming plane tree quivering in the wind, and my mind fills with the image of Clara's pouts.*

Will the tree's yellowish leaves whisper everything my present includes? A hundred faces, a thousand phenomena, and yet, underneath it all a single tone, like a constant vibration.

A call . . . a call from a crystal cage. Since our meeting on the Ile Saint-Louis I've been avoiding seeing the real Clara. Things seem simpler in Paridaiza. But for how much longer?

⌘

It has now proven to be true, continues Gagarina[x], that the experiment HI! wants to attempt—and which she already thought of weeks ago, sorry—has a good chance of succeeding, now that she has conducted a large-scale test of it. The blue lobsters and the plant life overrunning the vivarium in the Jardin des Plantes all carry a single eight-letter command: *Multiply*. As the Flipp brothers' crazy theories claimed it would, the implantation of a verbal code in the programming of these virtual species has functioned like a virus.

"And Malaner[x] hasn't said a word about it, even during pillow-talk with Mélodie[x]," smiles Clara[x], standing up. "I have a little surprise for everyone."

The apartment's doorbell rings. She opens it and ushers in two figures.

"This is my little sister, Mélodie[x]. You'll forgive her for looking a bit vacant; she's on Autopilot. And you all know her lover, don't you?"

There is a respectful, curious silence as Malaner[x] comes further into the room. Though young, he gives off an aura of maturity and self-confidence. As for Mélodie[x], she is a wave of pure sensuality.

"So what happens if someone eats one of the lobsters?" asks Ludwig[x] abruptly, turning toward the Nobel laureate's double.

"To be honest," replies Gagarina[x], smiling at Angelot[x], "we don't know the long-term effects of the multiplication code."

Personally, Malaner would say he's been having a lot of fun since joining forces with Gagarina to disrupt the workings of Paridaiza—it's a way of keeping control of a universe which, perhaps, had started to get away from him. And the unusual sensuality of an experienced young woman like Mélodie[x] would inspire even the most ambitious of men to break the rules.

Now Nuno[x] takes on the air of a sleepwalker, as Orante[x] comes out of Autopilot mode. He puts his dictionary on the floor, surprised by Gagarina[x]'s offhandedness.

"You have no idea of the long-term effects?" he repeats, a slight edge of anger in his voice. "So I'm just going to be a guinea pig?"

Gagarina[x] fixes him with a hard stare. "Have you heard of my Soulmate theory?"

"It seems somewhat outside the realm of your own experience."

"It's true that it is largely a mask I've put on in order to seem harmless to the Ultras. But not entirely. The question of the soul, you see, is not unrelated to that of the alphabetical virus."

A notebook filled with the scientist's vaguely esoteric sketches is now passed around the room from one HI! member to another.

"Graphically speaking, they're quite beautiful," says Ludwig[x], squinting uncomprehendingly at the drawings.

"My brother wanted to be a painter," says Mick[x], laughing, "but all he managed to do was rent an apartment on the rue des Beaux-Arts in Biearth-Paris."

"Can you be more specific?" interrupts Orante[x], addressing the Nobel laureate.

"The virtual has always existed. For centuries now, thanks to the evocative power of language, by means of symbols and images, humans have traveled through time and space, from body to body, from emotion to experience. The story of these travels is the true history of humanity. The story of souls. You are not the ones who need to be taught that a single word or image,

130

especially when repeated thousands of times, can move mountains."

The scientist falls silent, gazing neutrally at the faces surrounding her. She holds out a hand, and Mick[x] gives back her sketchbook. She rises, gives the silent Malaner[x] a friendly pat on the shoulder, and heads for the front door.

"That is what Soulmates are: bodies which the same set of symbols, or words, or images plunge into the same trance. You'll excuse me now; I have a great deal still to do. But I'll meet you on Monday morning at sunrise, in front of the southern gate of the Jardin des Plantes."

"What for?" asks Clara[x].

"We'll choose your magic word."

2
The ceremony

Anyone with even a slight knack for reading facial expressions would be able to see that, since the appearance of the blue lobsters, the eyes of many Biearth-Parisians have contained a mixture of euphoria and fear, like a premonition. Something irreversible is about to happen.

The vegetation in the parks has not overrun the city itself, but that is only because Parliament has called in several hundred Vivaguards to supervise the eradication of the out-of-control greenery. And at the same time, with Love Day getting closer and closer, Paris has become the most-visited city in Paridaiza for tourists. The capital is currently the premier destination for couples seeking romantic facades: the façade of Sacré-Coeur, the façade of the Hôtel Crillon, the façade of the Louvre, the façade of the Cathédrale Notre-Dame.

When you have grown up in Paris like Nuno has, you are usually less affected by the solid beauty of the city's monuments, whether authentic or simulated. On the contrary, however, it often happens that, rather than going home straightaway to connect to the game when he finishes his shift at the Arsenal library, Nunc heads for Notre-Dame. With its apse restored by Viollet-le-Duc and its twilit flying buttresses, it has always felt to him like the most stirring and emotional place in the real Paris. Maybe because of the powerful grace of its Gothic arches with their sharp curves. Maybe because of the garden that stretches to the foot of the apse, haloed at dusk with a mysterious aura. Maybe because this bastion of another era, this chimera knitted of bony lace—Nuno has sometimes seen it as ribs around a thoracic cavity, as if the cathedral itself were a lung—clings so majestically and determinedly to its place between two benign bridges.

The ramparts of the Ile de la Cité make it look like an unsinkable ship ready to face even the most destructive of tempests. Nuno and Clara took refuge here, one summer night.

It was three months after they had first met. The square behind the cathedral was closed, but they had scaled the fence, laughing, and there, sitting on a bench hidden among the trees, they had listened to "Casta Diva" from *Norma* on an mp3 player. The wavering flute, the murmuring male chorus, the ever-rising arabesques of Maria Callas's voice—Nuno had suddenly turned to Clara, filled with emotion:

"This melody . . . it's you."

She had gazed at him sadly, and after a long silence, had whispered:

"And I love no one but you."

She hadn't said *I love you*, but rather *I love no one but you*, and Nuno remembers thinking: *If that's true, then we are bound together for life.*

Tonight, not far from the square, Nuno slowly crosses the Saint-Louis bridge, alone. Clara's declaration of love seems a very long time ago. Avatar or not, simulation game or not, real or imaginary contact, the fact is that she is now also sleeping with his former best friend, which isn't doing anything to cure Nuno's jealousy of Malaner. It's Paris, too, he thinks; that recklessness, that neutral, practical immorality to which even the best souls sometimes fall prey here. *I am what I desire.* The consciences of many Parisians are like a boat more or less adrift, permanently pitching and tossing, unable to find a sure course or to spy the strait that will take it toward a greater, calmer ocean, with peaceful winds. Too calm . . . ?

⌘

Despite—or perhaps because of—Angelot[x], Mélodie[x] continues to occupy the mind of Orante[x], who is alone in his Vivarium apartment at the moment with his cat Pacha[x], who now lets out a questioning meow. It is late, and the small apartment is still and silent. After exchanging glances with the animal, Orante[x] turns on his stereo and opens a similibeer; perhaps a plaintive tango will help him along as he dilutes his thoughts with alcohol.

Pacha[x], to judge by the blank expression in his green eyes, isn't a fan of the subtleties of the bandoneon. He jumps onto the radiator, where he assumes a pose reminiscent of a sphinx who is also a music critic. When the second song begins, a quicker, lighter piece, a serene smile appears on his owner's face.

Romantic jealousy is stupid, Orante[x] thinks now; it's nothing but the projection of an obsessive action film onto the blank screen of absence. The absence of another and the absence of the self from the self; the absence of imagination, of self-discipline, of innocence; the absence of lucky chance, of temperance, or maybe of assistance, or exuberance, or connivance? The absence, even, of a leave of absence? All our problems stem from impatience in the end, he decides. But is impatience rooted in the conscience of our evanescence? For several days now he has felt more and more in love with Mélodie[x] every morning—which isn't the wisest course of action, considering that she's a simulated computer avatar.

He looks at the dictionary on the low table at the foot of his sofa-bed. On Monday morning his friends will probably ask him to open the book to a random page—it's a 2010 edition, containing 65, 761 words—and to proceed as blindly as a blue lobster, or his cat.

Pacha[x] chooses this precise moment to chase his own tail again, catching it for better or worse with his own claws. He engages in this absurd activity, preprogrammed though it is, every couple of days. Orante[x] watches him out of one eye, still leafing through the pages of the dictionary lying open on his stomach.

An idea has just occurred to him. What if he trains himself, over the coming days, to open the dictionary to the same page every time, in such a way as to appear random to his friends, simulating chance, and keeping their experiment from having completely anarchical consequences? It seems a difficult task at first glance, but if he works at it for several hours it might not be any more complicated than your average circus trick, like, say, juggling three balls at once.

But which word should he choose? Which word has the power, if the ripple effect is applied to it, to become truly magical?

On the other side of the mirror, Nuno can think of only one, the one which, since his last meeting with Clara, has sometimes made him want to cry, sometimes to scream, sometimes to laugh and dance the tango. Page 84. Left-hand column. Fifth word down.

Love.

⌘

The Soulmate fad is causing more and more outlandish behavior in Biearth-Paris as the date of Love Day approaches. Rumor has it, for example, that a young woman recently hit a man hard enough to draw similiblood when he declined to go for a drink with her. More and more characters are going out in public wearing antipollution masks, which hide much of the face and thus reduce the risk of "love at first sight".

Clara[x] and Nuno[x] are seated in the back of La Folie en Tête, a bistro in the Butte-aux-Cailles neighborhood. The almost village-esque tranquility of this part of the similicity makes it a haven of peace. A few long white flags, in the center of which is printed a blue lobster, hang from the windows. These cloth rectangles have begun appearing over the last few days, hung from the façades of buildings across the city; their exact meaning remains a mystery for now. The animal seems to have become a symbol of freedom, and more than one underground workshop has bowed to popular demand and begun printing these stateless flags. Neither the Vivarium Parliament nor the Biearth-Paris mayor's office has issued a reaction yet; they seem unable to determine whether the flags constitute a serious act of resistance. An initial survey of player opinions has revealed a split; for some of them the blue lobster has restored a sort of pagan faith in the ever-triumphant forces of nature and life, even in a simulated world. For others, the arthropod merely evokes something unusual and pretty, like a kind of mascot.

In any case, the phenomenon certainly won't be ignored by the authorities for much longer; the latest city hall count estimates tens of thousands of the blue crustaceans currently inhabiting the Seine, and what was formerly an extremely high-end delicacy is already featuring on hundreds of restaurant menus across Paris, even including two establishments in working-class Butte-aux-Cailles.

Clara[x] seems worried. She tries to share her doubts with Nuno[x].

"Do you remember what made me get involved with HI! in the first place?"

Nuno[x] wants to say, *The desire to get me back?* but he decides to take a different approach.

"Your hatred of mimicry and indoctrination?"

"That, yes, but also my taste for improvisation. But now I'm wondering if our project has too much at stake to take the risk of choosing a word randomly from the dictionary." She looks around warily before continuing, her eyes sparkling. "I actually think it would even be rather cowardly."

"How would you rather do it?" he asks, feigning surprise.

"We should all discuss it together, including Gagarina[x]. Each of us could suggest a salvational word, and we could debate them until we all agree."

"We can't change the rules like that at the last minute. We'll never agree on one word."

"Why not? Look at the blue lobster; it's obeying the code and multiplying. It works! We may only be sorcerer's apprentices, but because of Gagarina[x] and Malaner[x], we've got a shot at changing things on a grand scale, in Paridaiza, and maybe even on Old Earth too."

"Next you'll be telling me all we have to do is program the word *love* to turn the world into Paradise."

She smiles.

"I don't recall mentioning the word *love*. This isn't about you and me. You're too young to commit yourself."

"What if I'm the one who mentioned it?"

She is silent, inwardly pleased. Nuno[x] hesitates, then pushes on:

"You know, Magellan[x] is at home right now, in Autopilot mode. He's already opened and closed his dictionary a hundred times. He's trying to aim for the word *love*, but he's always a couple of pages off: *liking, loneliness, lemur*.

"I wish him luck."

⌘

The vivarium in the Biearth-Jardin des Plantes is an Art Deco edifice faithfully copied from the real 1929 structure, a one-floor building around a hundred square meters in area. It is located at the center of a menagerie where rare animals—Elliot's pheasants, Himalayan magpies, Kirk's dik-diks, Canadian geese, white-throated monitor lizards, Swiss gaurs, Siberian ibexes, Sichuan takin—, overly placid, overly spoiled animals, seem to be awaiting the Great Flood.

The interior of the vivarium is flooded with dazzling light that bounces in greenish tints off the checkered tile floor. Black-walled cubicles a meter wide and sixty centimeters deep, some of them more or less filled with water, each contain a palm-sized insect, a snake, a spider, or a crab. One of these glass cubes is currently hosting two pairs of blue lobsters whose sexuality has become positively indecent since Gagarina[x] manipulated their programming.

It is just before seven o'clock in the morning. Magellan[x]'s eyes sweep the room, aware of a strange closeness of atmosphere that he senses not just here, but in some parts of the Mirror Museum and in the mirodrome at Victoria's as well. Gagarina[x] has caused an enormous Persian carpet to be installed in the middle of the room, on which the members of HI! have gathered in a circle after removing their shoes. Their faces are solemn, except for that of Mick[x], who lets out a fleeting chuckle as he watches Orante[x] place his dictionary in the middle of the rug.

Gagarina[x] gestures at the geometric patterns on the rug, flower motifs in violet, indigo, and yellow, which are woven of a mixture of wool, silk, and cotton and somewhat reminiscent of the images in a basic kaleidoscope.

"You are sitting on the original garden of Paridaiza. I'm more attached to this carpet than I am my Nobel Prize."

"It's like a mandala," observes Mélodie[x], stroking the silky tapestry.

Since the group met up with Gagarina's double at the gate ten minutes ago, Orante[x] hasn't been able to keep his eyes off the couple formed by Mélodie[x] and Angelot[x]. Now he tries, and fails, to bite back an acerbic remark:

"Before we start, how can we be sure that Malaner[x] won't give us away to the Ultras? Don't you find it strange that none of us have been targeted by The Great Night?"

"Calm down," says a soothing voice. "This isn't the time. And anyway, it's thanks to Angelot[x] that we haven't been caught."

It is Kim[x] who has just spoken, the strongly-built young Asian woman with white-blonde hair, wearing a purple blouse and sitting alongside Gagarina[x]. Now Clara[x] puts her hand on Orante[x]'s arm, her eyes not leaving Nuno[x]'s face. Malaner[x] remains silent and focused, as if these romantic imbroglios have nothing to do with him. Gagarina[x] continues:

"Kim[x] is the top researcher at the Museum of Natural History, the large building you saw just inside the Jardin's main gate. Without her assistance, as I said, Malaner[x] and I would not have succeeded in our experiments on the plants and the blue lobsters. As it happens, she also has an idea of how we might be about to choose our virus word."

The Asian woman takes over, her voice hypnotic, her eyes fixed on the dictionary in the center of the carpet.

"Ludmila[x] tells me you're thinking of choosing a word at random."

Outside, the early-morning silence has just been shattered by the waking cries of the monkeys in the northern wing of the zoo.

"We aren't actually so sure if that's a good idea anymore," Clara admits.

"The monkeys are hungry," interjects Kim[x]. "We've only got about thirty minutes before the zoo staff gets here. Here's what I think: it makes more sense to pick a word for our virus that doesn't conflict with the carrier's personality, and it might even be best to pick a word he can have faith in. A word that resonates with his own destiny." She waits for Gagarina[x] to nod in agreement before continuing. "In my opinion, the fact that Magellan[x] believes he's descended from the great navigator is a sign we should pay attention to. Everything's happening as if a specific signifier has leapt across five centuries of History to land right in our laps. What's the first word that pops into your head when you hear the name *Magellan*?"

"'World'?" guesses Mick[x].

"My ancestor never made it all the way around the world," objects Orante[x]. "He was killed after crossing the Pacific, on an island, by angry natives. Only his scribe, the ship's clerk Pigafetta, made it back to Europe with a few other men on board the caravel *Victoria*. I don't think 'world' is our magic word."

"'Strait'!" exclaims Clara[x].

"The Strait of Magellan, the passage to the Pacific, the symbol of spiritual awakening," smiles Malaner[x], with a friendly thump to the shoulder of Orante[x], who starts as if he's just been roused from a long sleep.

⌘

Nuno[x] and Ludwig[x] walk back up the rue Lacépède in silence, gazing at the façades of the buildings. If you asked them to pick out the difference between the real Paris and Paridaiza-Paris, they'd be tempted to answer that the latter contains no empty space. It's a hazy impression, but it is as if space in the simulation game is full—too full—of pure activity, and thus, perhaps, of impure inactivity too. They pass beneath a white flag with a blue lobster on it. Glancing up, they see a little girl at a window, smiling down at them. Nuno[x] gives her a friendly wave.

"She's got such big eyes. The exact color of the sea."

"Did you know that on this street, in real life, two hundred years ago, the poet Nerval used to take his pet lobster for walks sometimes, with a blue ribbon for a leash?"

"You're kidding."

"No! He said lobsters were calm and serious and knew all the secrets of the sea. Plus they didn't bark."

"I wonder why so many players are relating to the lobster."

"Maybe because, underneath its hard surface, it has remained soft and delicate inside?"

They arrive at the place de la Contrescarpe and sit out on the terrace at the simili-Café des Arts. The glass windows in the surrounding buildings, some of them hung with flags, quiver and jerk in fits and starts. Around the small fountain in the center of the square, whose nine jets burble on a stone platform, a few cybertourists photograph themselves enthusiastically. A resident of the area placidly walks her chihuahua mix.

Suddenly a pot-bellied man in a chef's apron and hat bursts out of one of the restaurants in the square. Nuno[x] and Ludwig[x] watch as he babbles something feverishly to the people passing him. Something isn't right.

"He's the head chef at Le Delmas," explains their server, setting two serotonic coffees down on their table. "He's been that way since yesterday morning; just starts spouting off in all directions. But his boss doesn't dare sack him."

"Why not?"

"He makes one of the best blue lobsters in the city."

⌘

The next day, Orante[x] and the Flipp[x] brothers meet on the rue de la Gaîté at a quiet table in the Sunflower Café. There's a rumor going around Biearth-Paris that, for several days now, most of the people who have eaten one of the blue lobsters fished from the Seine have been acting abnormally. A ticket clerk at the Invalides metro station has been seen hula-hooping half-naked on the platforms. A teacher at the Biearth-Collège de France claimed in an interview this morning that human toenails contain trace amounts of gold, and that if every person on the planet agreed to sacrifice them, we could revive the economy. A fifteen-year-old boy has suddenly become able to read his classmates' lines of code through their clothing and similiskin.

Orante[x] frowns. "What about these reactions has anything to do with the code *Multiply*, though?" he asks his companions. "Shouldn't the people who've eaten the lobsters be having sex on every street corner instead?"

"It seems clear that Gagarina[x]'s virus affects humans differently," muses Ludwig[x]. "Maybe because of our inhibitions. It's like the conflict between social determinism and an out-of-control libido can only lead to a kind of insanity."

"If it's insanity, it's the sort people want," says Mick[x]. "The price of blue lobster went up 200% in just a few hours this afternoon. It's on the menu at thirty restaurants, at least, for three hundred paridollars a kilogram. The police have had to step in to keep people from poaching them; a bunch of students hung nets from the Pont Marie."

Orante[x] seems more and more anxious. "If Gagarina[x]'s experiment with the lobsters leads to a form of insanity, how can we be sure the code word *Strait* will bring about some kind of collective sublimation, like you say it will?"

"We could stop right now, it's true," admits Ludwig[x]. "Let bedlam continue to spread, and random chance take over again."

"But," retorts Mick[x], imitating his brother's tone, "what good is bedlam without a well-thought-out channel for all that sublimation?"

This is all becoming a bit too theoretical for Orante[x], who gazes silently at the sunflowers on the wall over the bar. The waitress, busily pulling a few pints of beer, darts a furtive smile at him. At the counter, conversations blur together and the faces seem carefree. He would love to believe this is all just a game, but something is missing. It's like his real life, when it comes down to it; he often finds himself lacking the key to understanding things. Or maybe he still just doesn't know how to read the clues that would enable him to unlock his own destiny.

Why did Nuno sign up for Paridaiza? Partly in the hope that it would help him figure out who he really is. And the idea of Love Day intrigued him, too. But now he feels even less sure of his own identity. Fewer and fewer things seem real, constant, present. Even worse, Clara has split herself into multiples, too. The last thing they need now is for the Magellan[x] virus to have disastrous side effects.

Mick[x] stands up, his face unusually grave. "I ate a blue lobster," he says.

"Can you just be serious for once?"

"I am serious. But apparently not for much longer."

II
The mustard seed

1
The Creal

With less than seven weeks to go until Love Day, Mick[x] has not been spared by what the media is now calling "Lobster Syndrome". In his fits of delirium he is convinced he's the reincarnation of Saint Genevieve, who protected Paris from invasion by the forces of Attila the Hun in the fifth century.

One of these attacks is happening at this exact moment, as Gagarina[x] and Kim[x] stroll through the gardens of the Champs-Élysées, watching Mick[x] and Orante[x], who walk ahead of them.

The two young men make a ridiculous pair. While the former chants at the top of his lungs, his face filled with disgust, that Love Day is heresy, Magellan[x] tries to spread the virus with which he was finally inoculated three days ago, attempting to bestow a Russian-style embrace on as many passing men, women, and children as possible, with middling success.

Gagarina[x] raises her eyebrows. "This isn't quite how I pictured the Revolution."

A few meters further along, rounding the corner of a hedge, the two women find Mick[x] by the Fontaine du

Cirque, whose lions spout water over four similimarble cherubs. Nearby, Orante[x] stands on a bench, his face raised to the heavens with an expression of ecstasy.

⌘

I'm sitting at Clara's piano. My mind is in a jumble, and it's both painful and joyous at the same time. She is standing next to me, her hand on my shoulder. With her other hand, she slowly keeps time.

When I asked her to give me piano lessons, she agreed without hesitation. And it's no ruse on my part; three times a week we get together at this instrument and everything seems simpler. We avoid talking about anything but music, even though, recently, our sessions tend to end in caresses.

I play scales with both hands simultaneously, being careful to use the fingering I learned a few days ago. I go slowly, and it's hard to breathe. It's strange; it's as if the piano's hammers are lifting up the spongy mass inside my skull.

The scales are elegant torture, even in C major. The third finger of the left hand has to fall on the A, and the fourth on the D. The third finger of the right hand always strikes the E and the fourth the B. Thanks to endless repetition of the scales in both directions using both hands at once, across four octaves, I'm getting better.

But not without bumps and relapses. Sometimes I experience a moment of absence at the keyboard, but Clara brings me back to reality. Or, at least, she tries to. Because the minute we're together, face to face, the invisible screen rises up between us, like a crystal wall. Is it my fault? Is it because I've played Paridaiza too much? Am I becoming a walking simulation?

⌘

That same evening, in the suburbs west of Biearth-Paris, not far from the Bois de Boulogne, Mélod_e[x] and Malaner[x] welcome the other members of HI! to their home. This is the second time they have used Angelot[x]'s house, which is many times larger than Mick[x]'s studio, as a meeting place. It was here, at the impressive computer array of Paridaiza's designer, that Magellan[x]'s coding took place a few days ago.

Malaner[x] is cordial but doesn't say much, as has been the case since he began living with Mélodie[x], who receives the group in the living room, decorated with rare music boxes and ancient mechanical marionettes. Gagarina[x] observes Mick[x]'s behavior out of the corner of her eye; he seems to be acting normally, for now. She has had no more success than the officially appointed scientific panel at finding an explanation for lobster syndrome.

But the main order of business for HI!'s members tonight is figuring out why Magellan[x] had a vision, at the Fontaine du Cirque, of a world he has spontaneously named the Creal. His face radiant, he is now handing drinks to Mélodie[x], Clara[x], and Kim[x], who ask him for a more detailed description of the images he saw.

"You're going to think I'm on drugs. The first impression I had was of being in a different universe from Paridaiza, maybe even an opposite one. There was a

151

kind of explosion, and I found myself in the corner of a sort of cloister, with a garden and a fountain."

"Did it look like a place you'd seen before?" asks Clara[x].

"Nothing was familiar, not even the smells, but at the same time I felt at home. I felt like I was inside a living kaleidoscope that would obey my commands. And it was as if there was honey flowing in my veins, an intense flow of desire. The path leading to the fountain formed a kind of maze that shifted and changed with every step I took. Shining, brightly-colored shapes were transforming constantly. I looked up and realized that the cloister didn't have any walls, only peristyle columns. How can I describe it? I felt like this world was my own creation in a way, but at the same time I was only the instrument of a divine harmony."

"Sounds like a hallucination," says Kim[x].

"I don't know. The cloister seemed profoundly real to me."

"What happened next?"

"I found myself at the foot of the fountain. I wanted to drink some of its water, which seemed to rise up as I came toward it. But suddenly, behind me, I heard Mick[x] shouting, just like he is now."

Indeed, Mick[x], suddenly stricken with one of his attacks, is in the midst of explaining to Gagarina[x] at the top of his voice how the grass is growing back wherever he steps. She tries to take his pulse but he jumps away, then kneels in a praying position.

"He'll be a lot better in ten minutes or so," says Nuno[x], looking for the first time at the small red box on a low table in Malaner[x]'s living room.

Angelot[x] approaches. "It's a replica of my first music box. You remember?"

Nuno[x] smiles. He turns the tiny crank and the minimalist tones of the theme from *Love Story* tickle the other guests' ears. Mick[x] soon straightens, calm now, as if the music has broken the spell over him. He comes closer, his face peaceful, and gestures toward the red box.

"May I?"

He turns the little crank again and leans back in relief, beneath the intrigued gazes of his friends.

⌘

In a corner of the living room, Gagarina[x] pulls Orante[x] aside and questions him. There is a malicious edge to her voice.

"But why Creal? Why did that neologism come to you so suddenly out of nowhere?"

"I don't know. I felt like I was entering the very depths of imagination and the heart of reality at the same time."

"And you felt good?"

He concentrates, searching for the right words. "Yes, it was truly a feeling of joy and confidence. I felt powerful, too, but with a gentle, harmonious kind of power."

"Was that the effect of a series of coincidences? Of synchronicity?"

"It was like I'd touched the very essence of my own being. I felt like everything was connected."

Gagarina[x]'s face lights up.

"This magical cloister with a fountain in the center . . . that exactly matches the description of what people called Paridaiza in the time of the prophet Zoroaster. The true Paridaiza, the one represented on my Persian rug, and not a gilded prison filled with greedy avatars. That is your Creal: the secret of the original Paridaiza."

"What secret?"

"None other than our spiritual roots. The yearning creativity that is the very essence of life. The imaginative desire that triumphs over our sinking, our collapse. The ancients called it the Poem of the Cosmos."

"You seem to know a lot about it. What does any of this have to do with the code word *Strait*?"

"The Creal is the strait."

"What do you mean?"

Gagarina[x] seems to be on the verge of admitting something, but she reconsiders, and places an index finger against Magellan[x]'s lips.

"Shhh . . ."

2
Le géant Anormal

With four weeks left before Love Day, two parallel phenomena are occurring in the Parisian capital of Paridaiza. Sales of Absolux music boxes have skyrocketed since Gagarina[x] revealed, in a message on her official website (earning her a raft of kudos from the Ultras), that the little musical machines are an effective remedy for lobster syndrome. No observer can deny that, upon hearing their tinkling sounds, the attacks suffered by those who have consumed the contaminated shellfish are immediately eased, no matter what tune is played: modern popular melodies such as *Love Story* work brilliantly, but so do Debussy's *Clair de lune* and Tchaikovsky's *Dance of the Sugar Plum Fairy*.

At the same time, a new crisis is emerging among the population, an even more worrying one in the eyes of the powers that be: some people have begun reporting visions of a half-real, half-imaginary world they all refer to as the Creal, of which they all consider themselves the ardent co-creators. The most outlandish descriptions evoke, pell-mell, riotous gardens and cathedrals of ivory draped in purple silk; glowing paper ladders; gleaming waterfalls composed of the letters of the alphabet; and geysers of Everything drenching deserts of Emptiness. It has occurred to one journalist to test the Absolux music boxes' efficacy against these new attacks—but without success.

HI! believes that visions of the Creal are connected to the *Strait* virus. Their crazy idea seems to have worked, at least in part; Magellan[x]'s code is indeed proving to be the key to a richer, more peaceful world. But the long-term effects remain to be seen, and it is uncertain whether *Strait* can have a large-scale impact, via its links to the Sensorium, on Old Earth.

What does Gagarina[x] think of all this? It's difficult to say. For two days now, no one has been able to reach her, or Kim[x].

⌘

When Nuno[x] joins his friends at the Sunflower Café, they are all wearing an identical expression of defeat. Malaner[x] and Mélodie[x] are absent, swamped with work these past few days in light of the unexpected craze for Absolux music boxes. On the table are an issue of *Happenings* and some empty glasses.

Nuno frowns. "Has Gagarina[x] been swallowed up by The Great Night?"

Clara[x]'s mouth twists. "It's only a guess at this point—maybe just paranoia—but I'm wondering if she and Kim[x] have betrayed us."

"We've been trying to contact them for three days," puts in Ludwig[x], picking up the newspaper. "They're

156

not answering, and this article, which might be wrong, of course, says that both the Vivarium and the press have been trying to get hold of Gagarina[x] too, but they haven't managed it either."

Nuno[x] is silent. At the corner of the table, Orante[x], on Autopilot, takes a gulp of similibeer.

"But," says Mick[x], "that could mean that Magellan[x] isn't a carrier of the *Strait* code after all, but another kind of virus, something a couple of traitors inoculated him with right under our stupid noses."

Something that is not quite an abyss opens up beneath Magellan[x]'s feet as he struggles to take this in, while Nuno[x] heads mechanically for the bathroom. He understands his friends' suspicions, but he feels torn between two opposing sensations. How would a person feel if they thought they were getting the name of a loved one tattooed on their chest, only to discover another name inscribed on the skin? Distracted by desire, seduced by Gagarina[x]'s charisma and Kim[x]'s strength and discipline, he would never have imagined that the two scientists could be bluffing, that their commitment to HI!'s plans only a lure. But if Gagarina[x] and Kim[x] have programmed another virus into his avatar, and this virus is what's causing the Creal experiences, how could he blame them for it?

"The Hazardous Intraterrestrials have been stripped of their revolution," declares Clara[x] theatrically. "The worm was in the apple when we stopped putting our faith in chance."

"Gagarina[x] would have betrayed us no matter what, if that was her intention," says Ludwig[x], his tone more restrained. "And we had no idea what she was doing to Magellan[x]. Even Malaner[x] didn't seem to understand it really, and he's supposed to be some kind of computer prodigy. Or he wasn't being honest with us either."

"We're jumping to some pretty hasty conclusions," Orante[x] says, trying to reassure himself.

"Did you notice the windows in the buildings on the rue de la Gaîté?" interjects Mick[x]. "There are more and more of those blue lobster flags appearing all the time. They remind me of Gagarina[x]'s huge Persian rug, the one with the original Paridaiza colors in it. How about we go and search her place?"

⌘

Learning to play the piano at twenty years old is like being a dumb little toddler all over again. Clara thinks I have some natural talent, but she's warned me against memorizing things, which is all too easy to do when you're practicing. We've been working on an early Rachmaninov polka recently, and sometimes my attention drifts away from the sheet music.

"You're playing by heart! Don't do that. Read every note," she corrects me.

By heart. Is that how I learned to say words? How I learned to live? By letting my body memorize, repeating more and more mechanically, cheating, even—rather than forcing myself to keep my attention fully in the moment?

"All these shortcuts, these habits we acquire . . . they only put us to sleep," insists Clara, a bit professorially.

Playing by heart, if I've understood her correctly, would be nothing but imitation. In music, as in life, it's just as difficult—perhaps even more so—to keep from imitating yourself as it is to keep from imitating others. Eventually, through giving ourselves over to mimicry, we stagnate. We run up against our memory's lack of imagination. We find ourselves curled up in the corner of our minds, trapped in our own mental comfort zone, gnawing away at the few indulgences that make us feel like we still exist, even as we have slothfully given up the effort of risk.

⌘

Malaner^x has become more and more detached from his duties in the Vivarium, though he remains a consulting member of Parliament. He is producing greater numbers of his music boxes every day, not just for the use of Biearth-Parisians who have eaten blue lobster, but now also for "export", the events in the capital city having launched an international craze for Absolux's tuneful little machines. Apart from the members of HI!, no one knows he is plotting against Paridaiza.

Despite the demands of his business, he has found the time today, at noon, to walk along the Biearth-Seine with Nuno^x, somewhere between the place de la Concorde and the Pont Neuf. Winter is coming, but the city is bathed in similisun, and the cold seems softened by the lack of wind and the quiet streets. But Nuno^x still seems worried:

"If they've erased Gagarina^x, it can't be much longer before The Great Night comes for all of us."

With less than five hundred hours to go before Love Day, there has still been no sign of the scientists. The members of HI! managed to get into her apartment, only to find that she has apparently left without taking her precious Persian carpet, which casts further doubt on the theory of a deliberate flight, much less a premeditated one.

Malaner[x], however, remains calm, almost as if he's found something out. "You're underestimating the protective filters I put in place. And you're underestimating Gagarina[x]."

"Pfft. It wouldn't be that big a deal to be banished from Paridaiza."

"Think again. A lot of people who've been playing for months and suddenly had their accounts closed by The Great Night are developing some actual problems in real life. Apathy, mental confusion, depression . . ."

"So we don't have a choice, then."

"We've made the choice—to change this world—and we need to follow through. We have to stay united."

Nuno[x]'s tone is ironic. "Oh, we're united, all right, you and me. We've even turned back into the kind of friends that share *everything*."

"Don't be petty. You know Clara loves you, and you're the one who's afraid of what she wants from you. And I love you too. Don't think I haven't noticed that you gave Orante Magellan[x] a name that's an anagram of mine."

"That isn't the only anagram of your name. There's also *Le géant Anormal*."

Angelot[x] bursts out laughing. "We've been here together before, do you remember? The real Pont Neuf, I mean. We were eleven and we pretended we were walking a tightrope on the parapet."

"Yeah. It seemed so big back then, but we weren't afraid. Makes me a bit dizzy now, though."

They watch the immense river flow beneath them in silence. Angelot[x] seems as if he is working up the nerve to say something important. Nuno[x] senses that events might be about to take a dangerous turn. They could give themselves over to the hyper-realistic illusion of Paridaiza and say that the water beneath their feet has coursed through the whole history of Paris, and will continue to do so. After all, the streets of this city have been demolished and rebuilt countless times over the centuries by a passionate people who is constantly reinventing itself. What makes the "virtual" any more illusory than the past?

On the other side of the screen, Nuno's breathing has slowed down. Even now, some days on Old Earth, he looks hard in all directions and sees only his own gaze reflected back by mirrored surfaces. At these times he clings hard to what is real. Walking toward the apse of Notre-Dame in the evenings, he runs his fingertips along the limestone handrail on the Pont Louis-Philippe, while the cells of his retinas capture the Seine's brisk undulations. Feeling . . .

He remembers how, even before the revelation of the Creal, in Old Paris, he has sometimes noticed intense but fleeting changes in his perception. On some nights, for example, the city seems to be lit up from unexpected angles, revealing, behind the fluted facades, the shadows of medieval hovels in their ghostly timbered corsets. These atemporal impressions, quicksilver and solid at the same time, feel as real to him, if not more, than the monoliths of carbonized rock, the riotous jumble of limestone and granite, sand and concrete, pipes and conduits, that sprout from the ground in daylight.

The most banal features of everyday life have always seemed strange to him. On a bus yesterday evening he looked for a long time at the face of a young woman with skin almost as smooth as that of the avatars in Paridaiza. Her lips are delivering phrases soaked in the milk of propriety to the girl next to her. Fascinated and almost horrified, he contemplated the ease with which this post-adolescent girl's mouth issued such formulaic words while her eyes looked robotically into the middle distance, calling into mind by contrast the curious gazes of childhood or the gleam in the beautiful eyes of the elderly.

Malaner[x] finally breaks the silence and looks Nuno[x] directly in the eye.

"Parliament figured out that someone has managed to graft a virus into the lobsters' algorithm. And in the lines of code of the avatars who have been having visions of the Creal, they've found a single word repeated in each line—a word that isn't *Strait*. They remembered Ludmila Gagarina's experiments on DNA and, fortunately without suspecting her or her avatar of being a pirate, they had the same idea we did, though too late and backwards. They decided to have her create an antidote, a counter-virus, to restore order. That's why they've kidnapped Gagarina[x] and Kim[x]."

Through the mind of the person controlling him, Nuno[x] suddenly remembers the recent conversation between Gagarina[x] and Orante[x]: "*The Creal is the strait.*"

He looks at Angelot[x].

"You've known what's going on since the beginning."

"Yes. That's the Magellan[x] code. Five letters. *Creal.*"

III
Render unto Caesar

1
The Commander

Periods of tolerance never last very long. Until now, Parliament thought it best to keep its distance from both lobster syndrome and the outbreak of mysticism that seems to lie beneath the psychedelic visions of the Creal. But this morning, with approximately four hundred hours left before Love Day, the Ultras announced that a Crisis Commander will govern the capital at this dangerous time.

A character lacking a complete biography, Alfred Menhir[x], a tall, fiftyish man whose rather old-fashioned allure includes a fine moustache and frequent quirking of his left eyebrow, has set up base-camp in Biearth-Matignon on the rue de Varenne, in the palace historically reserved for Prime Ministers. According to some rumors, Menhir[x]'s avatar is concealing a particularly wily former head of the Central Directorate of General Intelligence. It was he, apparently, who suggested the idea of sequestering Gagarina[x]. He has also ordered the police to arrest anyone speaking out loud the new *leitmotif* of the ecstasies of the Creal: "*The world is your creation!*"

The conditions of this second kidnapping are rather more comfortable for the Nobel laureate's double than they were in the HI! studio; she is being held with Kim[x] in a luxurious (though windowless) apartment in the basement of the Hôtel Biearth-Matignon. Her tinkering with the blue lobsters and her relationships with HI! and Malaner[x] have not yet been revealed. And, so far, Gagarina[x] and Kim[x] appear strangely unable to find a countermeasure for the *Creal* code.

What the kidnappers only half-suspect is the amount of time the two scientists are spending in search of a way out of their gilded cage. How to communicate with the outside world, though? Couldn't the real-life Gagarina and Kim, on Old Earth, simply disconnect from Paridaiza and alert Nuno or the real Ludwig and tell them to go to the press, for example? But provoking a reaction from HI!, any reaction, would risk attracting Godpreview's attention to the rebel group. It's never a good idea to give way to panic. And besides, Malaner[x] probably knows everything already anyway.

Indeed, on the evening of Sunday, December 10, 2012, Malaner[x] finds himself officially invited to Matignon, to be formally awarded the green-and-white-striped ribbon of the Order of Arts and Letters in recognition of his role, according to Alfred Menhir[x], in "maintaining public order" by means of his musical machines, which "do credit to French savoir-faire". Who knows what further havoc lobster syndrome might have wreaked on the population without Absolux and its music-boxes?

But now, who knows how far the Creal will spread? What is the danger that it will, through the Sensorium helmet, infect the real world?

⌘

These piano lessons might be what they say a session with a good psychoanalyst is like: they weaken me and break me down, but make me stronger in the end. The more my fingers do battle with the instrument's keys, the more my perception of the world seems to evolve and strengthen and become richer.

Now, when I walk down the street, I look around without wondering if I'm seeing reality or constructing it with the help of my thoughts of the future. I can feel my connection to the outside world in every cell of my body; my brain humming with ideas, impressions, and feelings that are more or less benign, my memory overflowing, the future present. Like reflections in a kaleidoscope . . .

I smile in these moments and say to myself that if Clara wants to have a child with a man-child, so be it!

⌘

Accompanied by Mélodie[x], Angelot[x] crosses the colonnaded entryway to enter the main courtyard of the Hôtel Matignon. Behind the grand façade, the building is designed to catch one's attention in three successive phases. The central pavilion boasts a slightly pretentious balcony adorned with leonine sculptures. The vestibule is capped by a low dome, inside which is a sumptuous reception room laden with hors-d'oeuvres and bottles of champagne, all prepared and labeled in Paridaiza's colors.

The couple is ushered into an adjoining room where some thirty guests are already assembled, some of whom will also be receiving honors tonight. As Mélodie^x surveys the finely reproduced woodwork, cornices, and stucco, Malaner^x recognizes the mayor of Paris, who is talking and laughing with Alfred Menhir^x.

An hour later, after he has finished giving a speech of thanks, intuition goads Malaner^x into leaving the radiant Mélodie^x to the other guests for a moment and wandering, not without curiosity, among the hotel's corridors. Suddenly, passing the half-open door of a video-surveillance office, he catches sight of a bald-headed man questioning his seated colleague in front of a dozen TV screens.

"Still not talking?"

"The old one? Eh, who gives a damn? It's the fat Chinese girl who gets me going."

Through the narrow opening, Malaner^x glimpses one of the monitor screens zooming in on the face of Kim^x. Just then, a voice speaks behind him.

"You're a lifesaver, Malaner^x," says the mayor of Paris, accompanying his surprise appearance with a cordial thump on the shoulder. "I was almost forced to step down, you know. The lobster had turned me into, shall we say, a bit of an exhibitionist. Fortunately, one of your little boxes came to my rescue before anyone outside City Hall found out about it. Just between you and me, it was never a very big deal anyway; the government is full of perverts. Elected officials have to have their fun, know what I mean? Ha ha!"

"Which box did you choose?" asks Angelot[x] with perfect smoothness, allowing the mayor to escort him back to the reception.

"*Orpheus in the Underworld*, by Offenbach."

"Ah, the French can-can. Did you know the dance was invented by the laundresses of Montmartre, based on the quadrille?"

"The lobster quadrille? Ha ha! But our Parisian girls have more delicate little pincers. Flexible muscles, flexible legs, flexible morals!"

"The splits *are* an eminently political dance . . ."

The mayor responds with a smile like the rictus of an old monkey before melting easily into the crowd of guests. Angelot[x] rejoins Mélodie[x] just as Menhir[x], holding the young woman's hands, is apparently wrapping up a monologue in praise of manual labor:

"I was just telling her, she has the hands of an artist," he says smoothly. "Congratulations, Malaner[x]."

"Nothing to do with me."

"No, he just reaps the rewards," says Mélodie[x] teasingly, slipping a piece of paper into her bodice with one hand and brushing Angelot[x]'s trouser-front with the other. The Commander looks surprised, while Malaner[x] grins like an idiot.

The couple leaves the hotel just before ten o'clock. HI! is having an emergency meeting at midnight in the suburban studio. Freeing Gagarina[x] and Kim[x] has become a matter of urgency.

But how?

"This might be helpful," says Mélodie[x], extracting the small, folded piece of paper from her décolletage. "A sneaky gift from the irresistible Alfred[x]. His private mobile number, I would think."

⌘

The next evening finds Magellan[x], fully dressed, cooling his heels in a bathtub on the top floor of a hotel on the rue des Beaux-Arts. All around him are large glass bowls filled with little pink and yellow bars of soap. Ludwig[x] and Mick[x] sit uncomfortably nearby, waiting.

On the building's zinc roof, Malaner[x] sits cross-legged in a misty similirain next to a short ladder, glancing from time to time at the broad Velux skylight through which he can see the bed on which Mélodie[x] is lying. She is wearing a violet silk dress printed with stylized robins, her fingers tipped with crimson false nails. Two roofs away, Nuno[x] and Clara[x] wait in Autopilot mode on the balcony of Ludwig[x]'s small apartment.

The night is dark and still. As expected, when she invited him to meet her in this room—in a tone few men would have been able to resist—, Alfred Menhir[x] had accepted immediately. A slave to his own sexual desire, the Commander seems to think nothing of visiting the companion of a man who has just been awarded an honorary distinction—but he is accompanied, all the same, by his two bodyguards when he knocks on the door of room 69 on the top floor of the hotel, his face partly hidden by a hat and dark glasses.

Mélodie[x] opens the door, sees the guards, and stiffens.

"They stay outside," she says firmly.

Menhir[x] looks like a sad-faced knight lost at a costume party. His gaze rakes the young woman's silk-clad body.

"Of course, princess."

The door closes. The government minister, impatient, rummages in the pockets of his jacket and extracts a small black box, which he exhibits with an oily smile.

"A portable version of the Pleasurium. Still in the testing phase."

He would prefer, if possible, to finish in a few minutes, savor the triumph of having conquered and penetrated one more woman—and what a woman!—and get back to his duties. But Mélodie[x] suddenly pushes him down on the bed. Her voice is a silken harpoon.

"Take your clothes off."

Trying unsuccessfully to conceal his excitement, Menhir[x] shrugs off his jacket and begins unbuttoning his shirt while the young woman, standing before the big bed, puts into practice part of what she learned in the mirodrome at Victoria's. Her eyes locked on his, she runs her hands down her breasts and slowly raises her silk skirt to her upper thighs.

The Commander blinks at the luminous vision that is now slowly approaching him. He takes off his pants, gazing circumspectly at Mélodie[x]'s fingernails, which are polished black, like the claws of a panther.

"Take off your boxer shorts and close your eyes."

He obeys, trying to give himself over fully to this rare moment in which he isn't playing the dominant role.

She opens a drawer on the nightstand and extracts a microsyringe of olanzapine, murmuring all the while.

"Keep your eyes closed . . . do you want to feel my mouth, or my fingernails?"

"Both," he breathes, like a newborn groping for his mother's breast.

Orante[x], scarlet with jealousy, chooses that precise moment to burst out of the bathroom and smash an enormous glass bowl over the head of Menhir[x], who barely has time to open his eyes before he is knocked unconscious. The noise is audible, though muffled, on the other side of the door of number 69; one of the bodyguards frowns.

"What are you doing?" demands Mélodie[x], keeping her voice low, turning in astonishment fo Magellan[x], as Ludwig[x] and Mick[x] emerge from the bathroom, disconcerted.

"Cry out!" whispers Orante[x]. "Cry out like you're in ecstasy!"

Even as she straightens her dress, Mélodie[x] obediently utters a lascivious cry that has the effect, on the other side of the door, of bringing an envious but reassured smile to the guard's face. Mick[x], meanwhile, goes through the Commander's clothes. Malaner[x] opens the Velux skylight and descends the ladder. Ludwig[x] looks at Menhir[x], grinning.

"I guess we'll never know the effects of olanzapine."

"Let's try to follow the plan now," says Malaner[x], inspecting the room's door.

In a few seconds they have hoisted the Commander's avatar onto the roof, while Mélodie[x] continues to groan loudly with pleasure before disappearing out the skylight behind the rest of the group. Their progress across the slippery roof is made perilous by the rain, but they reach Ludwig[x]'s balcony with their burden safely.

Gagarina[x]'s Persian carpet is ready. They lay the unconscious politician down on it. Mick[x] and Ludwig[x] then carefully roll the precious rug up with him inside. Once the procedure is complete, Alfred Menhir[x] is perfectly concealed.

The group creeps down the building's stairs with their package and, once out in the street, slide it into the back of a small moving truck just as, a few doors up, the two guards are finally forcing open the door of room 69 to find nothing but the minister's clothing scattered at the foot of an empty bed, as if Menhir[x] had somehow teleported out of the building.

As the van driven by Clara[x] leaves the center of Paris and heads for Malaner[x]'s studio, the first police sirens are heard, going in the opposite direction. In the back of the van, Mick[x] nudges Orante[x] and motions with his head toward the rolled carpet.

"Okay, you bowl-loving nutcase, please tell me all we have to do now is get some Creal into Menhir[x]'s guts."

"Just give the Commander a big smack on the lips," says Ludwig[x], laughing. "Hell of a plan for bringing around an anarchist revolution!"

Orante[x] feigns gloominess. "After what just happened, we're prime candidates for The Great Night."

"In that case, we have one last thing to take care of," puts in Malaner[x], seriously.

"What?"

"Yesterday, in my office in the Absolux tower, I indulged in a bit of remote-control fiddling with the programming of the mirodrome at Victoria's."

Mélodie[x] smiles. "Interested in sex shops, are you?"

"You could say that. I changed how the coin-slots work in the booths. If we end up in danger of being taken by The Great Night, we should be able to hide in the octagon. I'm not going to give you a programming lesson right now; let's just say, for simplicity's sake, that the coin-slots should be able now to identify The Great Night's lines of code as characteristics of an incompatible coin. We should be untouchable as long as we stay on the other side of the two-way mirrors."

Nuno[x] struggles to understand. "But we'll be trapped!"

"Yes, but we'll be able to disconnect at will, all at the same time."

"What difference does that make?"

"After all the time we've spent in Paridaiza, our brains are addicted. Deprivation that doesn't result from a voluntary, controlled decision could be catastrophic. But if we decide to jump together, concentrating on the Creal, we have a good chance of avoiding any side effects."

The little truck rolls along at an unhurried speed through the Bois de Boulogne. Mick[x] takes a sheet of paper out of his pocket and unfolds it.

"I found this document in Menhir[x]'s jacket. Web surfers aren't going to like this information very much."

⌘

Another piano lesson with Clara always reminds me that things are constantly changing; nothing is ever fixed. There are moments of discouragement. She says music can make you feel weightless, just as it can make you feel empty. You can feel almost dead at a keyboard.

Sometimes I'm tempted to disconnect permanently from Paridaiza, alone, unsupported, despite the risk and danger, and to suggest that Clara do the same thing. But isn't it just as dangerous, and cowardly, too, not to see this through to the end?

Has the game gone too far, or not far enough? Yesterday I told her I was willing to have a baby with her. She didn't go wild with pleasure; just looked at me, with tears in her eyes, and said thank you. I felt alive, and so close to her. The crystal wall had melted away.

IV
Apocalypse

1
December 21, 2012

Consternation!

Ulceration!

Stupefaction!

Circumspection!

Emotion!

Affliction!

Incomprehension!

Dissension!

Regression!

Machination!

Congestion!

Dispossession!

Oppression!

Detestation!

Glaciation!

Revulsion!

Convulsion!

Revolution! Over the past few days, violent protests have broken out in Biearth-Paris against the government, which have been put down only with great difficulty due to the diversity of the protesters, who range from high-level executives to scantily-clad teenagers but who are all united in their rejection of Love Day. The populace has reacted angrily to the content of the report found by Mick[x] in Menhir[x]'s pocket and subsequently released by HI! to the media. The document clearly states that tests of the Amorium have shown it to be effective for no more than a few weeks, after which 49% of test subjects progressively shifted from empathy to hatred intensified by resentment, and even violence.

Love Day has now, of course, been postponed to an indeterminate date in the future, according to a statement given to *Happenings* this morning by Alfred Menhir[x], five days after his liberation via military operation. The few visions he has had of the Creal since being (generously, but not without repulsion) kissed by Orante[x] seem to have softened his world view, and now when he looks in the mirror he no longer sees only a man who enjoys domination, but a romantic as well. However, the decision to put the Amorium on the back burner has delayed his resignation, at least for now, given the unrest currently reigning in the streets of the capital to the great astonishment of international observers, who can't remember being so surprised by French behavior since the late 1960s. What Menhir[x] doesn't know, though—and neither, this time, does

Malaner[x]—is that Parliament has an alternative plan for December 21st . . .

Five days ago, the hostage-exchange of Menhir[x] for Gagarina[x] and Kim[x], scheduled to take place in the forecourt of the Biearth-Arsenal Library, did not go as planned. All the members of HI!, including Malaner[x], were arrested by police after a chaotic high-speed chase among the library's stacks. They were then secretly placed under surveillance inside Malaner[x]'s studio, the latter having been summarily dismissed from all his duties within the Vivarium.

The only positive aspect of the HI! debacle is that it has, so far, kept Parliament from making an example out of them via The Great Night, so as not to arouse mass sympathy for these rebels by turning them into martyrs—particularly Gagarina[x], whom everyone now knows is behind the Magellan[x] code, that strait toward the Creal.

However, Parliament is rapidly losing control of the situation; two days ago, the Vivaguards assigned to monitor the prisoners in Malaner[x]'s studio deliberately abandoned their post—but not before asking for an autograph from Gagarina[x], leaving the doors open, and walking away chanting: "The world is our creation!"

Indeed, the propagation of Creal syndrome bears most of the responsibility for the apparent lawlessness now reigning over Biearth-Paris. It is not uncommon, in fact, for the same character to have two or three visions in less than 24 hours. Most of the population seems to have lost interest in almost all of the entertainments available for purchase in Paridaiza, abanconing themselves instead to creative ecstasy and the pleasure of telling others about their waking dreams. There are even rumors of groups experiencing collective visions by holding hands.

Newspapers are now being published only sporadically, and there is nothing on similitelevision except prerecorded programs and reports of Crealist trips. Public transportation has become unreliable, and criticism of the Ultras is growing by the day, as is the fear, among the most clear-headed players, that Parliament will implement a final solution to the anarchy.

Even the economy has ceased functioning in Biearth-Paris except in the most minimal terms, and it is estimated that 70% of employees have stopped going to work without any prior warning of a strike. Supermarkets are looted regularly with the amused complicity of cashiers, and vehicles are abandoned on public roads. Last night's issue of the *Biearth-New York Times* bore the headline "Biearth-Paris: surfing the Apocalypse".

In the real Paris, the one on Old Earth, some observers have begun to notice a new sense of freedom in the air, albeit greatly dulled by the filter of the Sensorium . . .

⌘

The sun is shining in a cloudless sky and the winter air lacks its usual sharp edge. It is four o'clock in the afternoon on December 21st. Sitting on the steps of the Opéra Garnier, Nuno^x, Clara^x, and their comrades are awaiting sunset, which is expected to occur at 4:56.

Gagarina[x] has donned a flowing red wig to avoid being recognized. Over the past few days they have often caught her smiling, as if her dreams of scientific mysticism are coming true: the birth of a new era.

The city looks like a liberated war zone. Pedestrians walk past in joyful, unpredictable little groups. The Place de l'Opéra is bathed in a sort of decadent, twilight-of-the-Empire glow. Several hundred cars have stopped in the street, their drivers' faces raised skyward. It is 4:50. Kim[x], seated on a step next to Magellan[x], puts a comforting hand on his shoulder and whispers in his ear:

"I've got a bad feeling about this; how about you?"

For more than ten years now, occult forums and esoteric books have been putting forth the most improbable theories about today's date. Gagarina has some of them listed on her website; besides the famous Mayan prophecy, a message hidden in the Torah supposedly warns that the earth will be hit by a comet and explode. Other, more fantastical sources predict the arrival of extraterrestrials, particularly from the Pleiades—supposedly the creators of our own DNA—but also Sirians, Arcturians, and the less well-worn Zetas of Reticulum.

It is 4:57. The sun should have set by now.

Instead, the city suddenly seems more brightly illuminated.

The gazes turned toward the sky have seen nothing, but those people who now look down at eye-level witness a spectacle that defies understanding.

The avatars in the Place de l'Opéra, and indeed all over Paris, stand frozen, wide-eyed. All around them the buildings, the pavement, most of the objects—almost anything composed of inorganic materials—have just transformed into crystal. Everywhere there is only transparent architecture, gleaming angles of stone, dazzling reflections, an almost unbearable purity of beauty. Paris has never been so deserving of the moniker "City of Light". An awestruck silence seems to shrink time into a sublime hologram.

Nuno[x] and Clara[x] stand, transfixed, as if floating on the steps of quartz and pure silica. Their comrades' faces all wear the same expression of amazement. Gagarina[x] has clasped her hands in front of her mouth in an involuntary prayer. It is only after several moments that Mélodie[x] is able to summon words:

"It's incredible . . . but I feel very heavy all of a sudden."

"Me too, and . . . I'm having trouble breathing," murmurs Ludwig[x]. "Maybe . . . the world has stopped turning? Or started turning in the opposite direction . . ."

"It hurts," groans Mélodie[x] now.

"We may be transforming into crystal too," says Gagarina[x], her features contorted with the effort of speaking.

Magellan[x] tries to hold back a grimace of pain. "But why?"

"All of this . . ." says Malaner[x], ". . . it looks like a deactivation of hologram opacity, a manipulation of the Sensorium. It's basically the game without color

. . . without the . . . substance effects, you see. A skeleton-Paridaiza."

But, at five o'clock, the group suddenly becomes lighter again. The feeling of heaviness in the blood in their veins fades away. Yet the city remains crystallized. Some buildings are so transparent that the people are visible inside them as pallid shapes wearing astonished expressions. Nuno[x] turns anxiously to Gagarina[x].

"Do you have a better explanation for this?"

"I'm no crystal ball reader."

Mélodie[x], contemplates the glittering façade of the opera house, this Second Empire building where she has always dreamed of singing. The translucent stone reflects the light in countless mirror-like facets descending the loggia like a waterfall. It's beautiful, even sublime. But what trap is all this beauty concealing?

⌘

A new rumor now begins to make its way through the city streets, infiltrating the consciousnesses of the dumbfounded players. From street to street, the word circulates among the distressed crowds. Witnesses are reporting that, beyond the city limits of the capital, everything is gone. An impenetrable blackness, contrasting with the brightness of crystal: The Great Night is at the gates of Biearth-Paris.

For now it seems to be moving slowly, a centimeter at a time. But any characters who have ventured outside the city have been quickly swallowed up by the nothingness.

Behind Malaner[x] and Nuno[x], the group has finally forced itself to start moving again, and walked down the avenue de l'Opéra to the Louvre. No one can claim that the building clashes with its pyramid anymore; through the transparent walls and floor the multicolored similipaintings can be seen, strangely unchanged; it's as if they are floating, inalterable, in a glass jewel-case, or are bright brushstrokes in some immense tableau.

Biearth-Paris seems to be standing apart from the rest of the universe. No further contact is possible with the rest of Paridaiza; communication devices no longer function in their new crystalline forms. Yet, in the museum lobby, the soda machines continue to disgorge cans of simili-7up when glass coins are inserted.

"The mystery of machines," remarks Ludwig[x], wondering if it's safe to drink the orange juice he has just bought in a transparent can.

Nuno[x] stares, astonished, at the Rubik's cube he has just pulled from his pocket, the mineralized faces of which gleam faintly in the twilight. Gagarina[x], meanwhile, walks toward the Seine, drawn by intuition:

"I bet the blue lobsters haven't been touched, so that people will start eating them again," she says. "It's typical. On one hand, they encourage madness; on the other, they quash rebellion."

2
Sacré-Coeur

Late in the afternoon of December 24, 2012, alone with Mélodie^x, Magellan^x is irritated by his own silence, which he has maintained for several moments now, watching her cry. She is cradling a crystalline music box in her hands.

They have been sitting for almost an hour now on the roof of a green truck just outside the simili-Bois de Boulogne, in a children's play area. Behind the trees, beyond the city limits, the yawning blackness stretches away, like the depths of a bottomless well. Only a few hours ago, some three kilometers from here, Malaner^x's suburban studio and the Absolux music-box workshop still stood—but now they are gone, engulfed in a non-place darker than a night without hope.

Orante^x's mind buzzes with words and emotions that swarm and collide as if his head is a pinball machine with an awkward new player controlling the flippers. His navigator ancestor, Magellan, knew that the highest ambition to which a man can aspire is to be a beacon for others. But right now, Orante^x has no idea what to say to Mélodie^x—let alone, through her, to Clara.

In less than three days, Paris has been plunged into chaos, despite attempts at putting survival strategies in place. While the supermarkets have rapidly been emptied of any organic foodstuffs spared from crystallization—an ambiguous favor in the torture imagined by the Vivarium Parliament?—it is becoming clear that the main alimentary resource will soon be confined to the flesh of the blue arthropods now numbering in the hundreds of thousands in the Biearth-Seine.

The crystallized mechanisms of Absolux's music boxes have ceased to work, and lobster syndrome has resurged with a vengeance; anyone who has not been rendered mentally unbalanced by the strangeness of recent events will probably become so the moment they ingest one of the crustaceans. Many, terrified by the growing uncertainty in the city, have already forsaken the depleted grocery-store aisles to seek refuge in the consumption of blue lobster, in the anxious, despairing manner of drug addicts. The more reasonable citizens, though still abstaining from consumption for now, are no less disturbed and unsettled by the feeling that the world is slowly collapsing in on them.

Biearth-Paris, thinks Magellan[x], might soon resemble nothing so much as a luxurious insane asylum floating in the middle of nowhere; a shimmering cage filled with inmates whose incoherent babbling echoes off a million crystal facets. And then it will all be gone, and order will regain the upper hand. Unless the Creal can somehow vanquish The Great Night . . . ?

The angry mob that marched on the Hôtel Matignon on the night of December 21st found the place all but deserted, save for the sorry presence of one Alfred Menhir[x], who was in no fit state for anything. Shut away in his room, on his knees in nothing but boxer shorts, his moustache shaven off, half-blinded by the over-brilliance of crystal gleaming around him, the poor Commander had finally dissolved in tears, whimpering *I'm just a little transparent boy . . .*

It often seems like you can never really know the true personality of some politicians, muses Orante[x]. But that's because they don't even know themselves.

Mélodie[x] sighs.

"The Great Night is coming faster and faster; I can feel it. We should probably just disconnect and pray there won't be any side effects. I'd prefer not to be a depressive."

Magellan[x] takes the young woman's hand. "We've got to stay united. We still have the Creal. We'll find a way. Shall we go back to Sacré-Coeur now?"

The widespread rumor now is that no one who has suddenly disconnected from the game out of fear has been able to handle their return to Old Earth, where there have already been a number of suicides blamed on Paridaiza. Recently, some Biearth-Paris citizens have started searching for Gagarina[x], convinced that she will know how to help. But even if anyone had recognized the Nobel laureate's avatar in the street despite her wig, she wouldn't have had a clue what to tell them.

Gagarina[x], too, is anxious.

She sits beside Malaner[x] on the steps of the Sacré-Coeur Basilica. Neither of them can look away from the black horizon advancing slowly toward them like a storm on the edge of the vast, crystalline landscape.

⌘

Nuno[x] and Clara[x] have no idea how long they've been walking. Right now they are on their way back up the rue des Martyrs, transfixed by the mesmerizing gleam of the buildings' transparent façades. The other avatars they pass are invariably in groups of between four and ten, almost like packs. Many of them are pushing shopping carts full of live blue lobsters, having chosen madness as the easiest route to salvation.

Nuno[x]'s pocket bulges with the hard square shape of his crystallized Rubik's cube.

"You should throw that thing away," Clara[x] says. "People will think you don't care about what's happening."

"I feel like you're blaming me for dragging you into all of this. But it has helped me to see just how much I love you. I've been so selfish."

Clara[x], laughs, maybe to hide her embarrassment. "Do you really think this is the right time for this conversation?"

But he persists. "What if Clara and Nuno make a life together on Old Earth, far away from computer keys and much closer to piano keys? I very much want to give you that child . . ."

"You're absolutely sure? Why now?"

"To tell him, or her, about everything we've experienced in the last few months, for one thing. And to try to raise a person without duplicity, someone who won't be dependent on anything but his or her own creativity."

"If you're so creative, find us a way out of this that doesn't involve too much pain."

Reaching the Place du Tertre, the couple sees a large crowd of people gathered around a weeping woman. Her hair in disarray, she is repeating the latest rumor, which has begun rapidly making the rounds within the past hour, borne on a wave of panic: The Great Night has crossed over the boundary created by the ring road, swallowing up everything in its path as if the universe is turning back on itself angrily, like a glove. Paris is now shrinking by a few dozen centimeters per second.

Nuno[x] and Clara[x] run toward the forecourt of the basilica. There they find their seven comrades lined up on the steps, eyes fixed worriedly on the horizon. From this height, it can be seen with the naked eye that the cloak of darkness encircling the capital is rapidly closing in.

"Weather's closing in, as they say," remarks Mick[x], in a tone he probably meant to be lighter. "Shall we make a move?"

Malaner[x] stands up. "There's still the mirodrome at Victoria's, and the protective block I put on the coin-slots."

"Ah, yes, the golden tomb," sighs Mélodie[x].

"Let's have some faith in Angelot[x]," says Gagarina[x] bracingly. "This is our last hope. Maybe something will happen there to help us fight The Great Night."

Magellan[x] suddenly speaks up, his voice fierce. "Then let's give ourselves a *nom de guerre*, before our final battle!"

"Good idea," says Clara[x], smiling and counting her friends. "HI! is an army battalion now, and we have to trust in the Creal. The Victoria's mirodrome will be our strait to freedom, to the light of the Pacific!"

"To the Great Midday," Malaner[x] grins.

Sitting there on the steps overlooking the capital, looking south, Nuno[x] tries to make out the transparent rooftop of the Arsenal Library in the distance. Then he stands and declares, heroically: "The Arsenal of Midday shall not be archived!"

⌘

The distance between Sacré-Coeur and the rue de la Gaîté is a nearly seven-kilometer straight line that takes one person around ninety minutes to walk, encompassing the rues Bochart-de-Saron, Châteaudun, Saint-Anne, the Place du Carrousel, and the bridge of the same name on the Right Bank, and then the rues du Dragon and du Cherche-Midi on the Left Bank. For a group of nine avatars, two of which are on Autopilot, progress is obviously much slower, all the more so because it's difficult to get your bearings in the city now that it has become crystallized; all the buildings seem to be reflections of one another, the ground is slippery in some places, and the diamond-like beauty of the views is such that the walker, dazzled, is often tempted to stop and stare.

Moreover, every time one of the group members is seized with a vision of the Creal—which happens along the way to Mick[x], Clara[x], and Kim[x], they lose several minutes waiting for the spell to pass.

All along the way to the mirodrome they pass Parisians gripped more and more tightly by sheer panic, running in their hundreds toward the city center. According to rumor, The Great Night has now reached the National Library to the east, the Champ-de-Mars to the west, the Place de Clichy to the north, and the rue d'Alésia to the south. Some desperate souls are claiming that the cathedral of Notre-Dame will be spared, and consequently the church has never been so crowded with "miscreants". Others consider the Panthéon a more certain refuge, topped with and guarded by the protective statue of Saint Genevieve as it is.

"We're not moving anywhere near fast enough. Let's run!"

Hurrying in the ever-more-determined footsteps of Magellan[x], the group turns down the rue du Dragon toward the rue du Cherche-Midi.

The Great Night is poised to absorb a large portion of the Montparnasse Cemetery that includes the tombs of Sartre[x], Beauvoir[x], and Duras[x] and nearly those of Tzara[x] and Baudelaire[x], and is uncomfortably close to the rue de la Gaîté. A few moments later the nine comrades hit that street at a run, heading for the sanctuary of Victoria's.

But, as they pass the Mirror Museum, Nuno[x] stops. "Keep going," he calls to Clara[x]. "I'll catch up with you in a minute."

⌘

The museum is open, though empty. Inside, all is silence and shadow. Nuno[x] goes into the funhouse mirror room, watching his outline multiply, then lengthen and widen.

He knows his friends are waiting for him, that he needs to do this quickly. But do what? Why this uncontrollable desire to bid farewell to the mirrors? He fingers the Rubik's cube in his pocket, takes it out and holds it flat on the palm of his hand. There are still molten swirls of color in the milky transparency of the crystal.

He wants to purify himself one last time, he realizes. To empty out the last dregs inside him here. He concentrates, grimaces, feels a kind of causeless guilt rise up inside him, the residue of shame and anger. He opens his mouth silently, as if to breathe out the last particles of wrongness inside him.

He screams.

He screams from deep within himself, a howl both human and animal at the same time, like an exorcism, an expelling from his body of the dead husks of vanished demons. He suddenly catches sight of himself in a mirror, and is frightened, just for an instant. He didn't recognize himself. He bursts out laughing.

He takes a few steps forward. Armed with his cube, he launches himself at a convex mirror, hammering at it until the crystal explodes into glittering slivers. There is pain in his right hand. His fingers are bloody, but the sight of this real-false blood amuses him. He begins hacking at another mirror, this one concave, yelling like a barbarian, weeping with joy.

Silence descends again.

He feels profoundly calm. He sits down on the floor, and then thinks he hears a familiar voice.

"Nuno[x]!"

Clara[x] has come back for him. She crouches next to him. He scrutinizes her lovely face. For the first time, he feels like he can see Clara's soul behind her double's eyes. It is like a warm, mischievous twinkle, a gleam that lights the mirrors around them. They sit silently for a few seconds, looking at one another among the crystal shards. Then she smiles, and asks, softly:

"Do you know the story of the Land of Emptiness?"

He shakes his head, his eyes never leaving hers. She kisses him gently on the lips, then continues:

"Once there were two worlds, separated by a strait. One world was called the Land of Emptiness, and the other was called the Land of Fullness. It was a place of abundance, full of incredible beings. New forms of plants and animals and souls were constantly being created there, as if through spontaneous generation. The Land of Emptiness, on the other hand, was arid, almost like a desert, and populated by needy people living in duplicity."

Nuno[x] smiles. She goes on, passionately:

"The strait was wild and dangerous, and very few dared to attempt a crossing. Yet from time to time, an inhabitant of the Land of Emptiness managed to get to the other side on a makeshift raft. And these people always brought back a few seeds which, planted in the desert, eventually created an oasis, where birds came to rest in the trees."

"Robins?"

"Yes, robins. And so a fountain sprang from the parched ground. Amidst the emptiness, these fleeting oases weren't enough to make people forget the desert, but they gave an idea of the lush lands on the other side of the strait. It was enough to make the thirsty people feel an unstoppable desire for a better world."

She stands up and holds out her hand.

"Should we join the others, or disconnect?"

He takes her hand and stands, smiling, his heart free and full of love.

"We'll join the others. And disconnect."